THE ENCHANTED WORLD OF HONEY MOON

DOUBLE TROUBLE

by

Suzanne Brooks Kuhn

with Joyce Magnin

Illustrations by Becky Minor
Based on the artwork of Christina Weidman

Created by Mark Andrew Poe

rabbit  publishers

Double Trouble (The Enchanted World of Honey Moon)
By Suzanne Books Kuhn
with Joyce Magnin
Created by Mark Andrew Poe

Rabbit Publishers
1624 W. Northwest Highway
Arlington Heights, IL 60004

Illustrations by Becky Minor
Based on the artwork of Christina Weidman
Cover and Interior Design by Lewis Design & Marketing

ISBN: 978-1-943785-22-3

10 9 8 7 6 5 4 3 2 1

1. Fiction - Action and Adventure 2. Children's Fiction
First Edition
Printed in U.S.A.

"Sometimes I carry your stuff
and other times I carry you."
— *Turtle*

TABLE OF CONTENTS

PREFACE

Halloween visited the little town of Sleepy Hollow and never left.

Many moons ago, a sly and evil mayor found the powers of darkness helpful in building Sleepy Hollow into "Spooky Town," one of the country's most celebrated attractions. Now, years later, the indomitable Honey Moon understands she must live in the town but she doesn't have to like it, and she is doing everything she can to make sure that goodness and light are more important than evil and darkness.

Welcome to *The Enchanted World of Honey Moon*. Halloween may have found a home in Sleepy Hollow, but Honey and her friends are going to make sure it doesn't catch them in its Spooky Town web.

FAMILY

Honey Moon

Honey is ten years old. She is in the fifth grade at Sleepy Hollow Elementary School. She loves to read, and she loves to spend time with her friends. Honey is sassy and spirited and doesn't have any trouble speaking her mind—even if it gets her grounded once in a while. Honey has a strong sensor when it comes to knowing right from wrong and good from evil and, like she says, when it comes to doing the right thing— Honey goes where she is needed.

Harry Moon

Harry is Honey's older brother. He is thirteen years old and in the eighth grade at Sleepy Hollow Middle School. Harry is a magician. And not just a kid magician who does kid tricks, nope, Harry has the true gift of magic.

Harvest Moon

Harvest is the baby of the Moon family. He is two years old. Sometimes Honey has to watch him, but she mostly doesn't mind.

II

Mary Moon

Mary Moon is the mom. She is fair and straightforward with her kids. She loves them dearly, and they know it. Mary works full-time as a nurse, so she often relies on her family for help around the house.

John Moon

John is the dad. He's a bit of a nerd. He works as an IT professional, and sometimes he thinks he would love it if his children followed in his footsteps. But he respects that Harry, Honey, and possibly Harvest will need to go their own way. John owns a classic sports car he calls Emma.

III

Half Moon

Half Moon is the family dog. He is big and clumsy and has floppy ears. Half is pretty much your basic dog.

FRIENDS

Becky Young

Becky is Honey's best friend. They've known each other since pre-school. Becky is quiet and smart. She is an artist. She is loyal to Honey and usually lets Honey take the lead, but occasionally, Becky makes her thoughts known. And she has really great ideas.

Claire Sinclair

Claire is also Honey's friend. She's a bit bossy, like Honey, so they sometimes clash. Claire is an athlete. She enjoys all sports but especially soccer, softball, and basketball. Sometimes kids poke fun at her rhyming name. But she doesn't mind—not one bit.

Brianna Royal

Brianna is also one of Honey's classmates. Brianna is different from all the other kids. She definitely dances to her own music. Brianna is very special. She seems to know things before they happen and always shows up in the nick of time when a friend is in trouble.

IV

FOES

Clarice Maxine Kligore

Clarice is Honey's arch nemesis. For some reason Clarice doesn't like Honey and tries to bully her. But Honey has no trouble standing up to her. The reason Clarice likes to hassle Honey probably has something to do with the fact that Honey knows the truth abut the Kligores. They are evil.

Maximus Kligore

V

The Honorable (or not-so-honorable depending on your viewpoint) Maximus Kligore is the mayor of Sleepy Hollow. He is the one who plunged Sleepy Hollow into a state of eternal Halloween. He said it was just a publicity stunt to raise town revenues and increase jobs. But Honey knows different. She knows there is more to Kligore's plans—something so much more sinister.

THE LONG WEEKEND

Sleepy Hollow, Massachusetts is not like any other town in America, possibly the entire world. Sleepy Hollow is a town that got its calendar stuck on one day, one frightful day— Halloween.

Long, long ago, before Honey Moon was even born, the mayor of the town enlisted the forces of darkness to plunge Sleepy Hollow into a state of forever Halloween. For most of the people, this came as a great boon because it was at a time when their businesses were not doing so well. Almost overnight, tourists began flocking to the small town in search of Halloween and, of course, the infamous marauder of Sleepy Hollow, the headless horseman.

Not wanting to disappoint visitors, Mayor Kligore had a huge, bronze statue of Washington Irving's headless horseman installed right, smack dab in the middle of the town green. Tourists love to have their pictures taken with the heinous horseman. But that wasn't all— every business, every shop, and nearly every home took on Halloween. They decorated their windows with spiders and bubbling black cauldrons and icky spider webs. Everywhere you looked, scarecrows adorned lawns and plastic ravens perched on fences. Even the air smacked of Halloween with the sweet, nutty, and spicy aroma of autumn—even in February.

While most of the townsfolk embraced the change and went along with all things Halloween, one girl, Honey Moon would rather turn the other way and look on the light side of life. But

2

that's not always easy, especially when you went to school with the mayor's daughter, Clarice Kligore. Clarice enjoyed following in her father's footsteps and creating trouble wherever she could. Sometimes even double trouble.

Honey Moon raised her hand. "The answer is twenty-seven," she said.

"That's correct," Mrs. Tenure said.

Honey smiled. She loved it when she had the answer. She especially loved it when she was the first one to raise her hand. Not that Mrs. Tenure always called on her. Sometimes she waited for another student to get the answer. But still, Honey always felt good when she solved a problem.

Mrs. Tenure turned toward the white board. She wrote another problem, but this time she used her red marker. That usually meant it was an even more difficult problem to solve.

Honey copied the problem into her workbook. But before she could even get started

1.) $(2+7) - (4x$

4

on the solution, Honey saw Clarice Kligore toss a small paper bat across the room. Honey shook her head. Clarice. Always up to something. Honey knew that Clarice did not share Honey's enthusiasm for school, but Honey wished that Clarice would at least try to behave.

Mrs. Tenure wrote five more math problems on the board. They were all written in red ink. All the students groaned.

"Now, now," Mrs. Tenure said. "I know you are all excited to get started on your long weekend, but we still have work to do and twenty-five minutes to get it done."

A long weekend. Honey was especially looking forward to this one. The Mummy Mate Scouts planned to spend Saturday night in the old Poe house out on Shocky Rock Street. It was an annual event, and each year the girls who were working on their Courage Badge had to spend one night in the old, supposedly haunted, mansion.

This year, Honey, Claire Sinclair, and Becky Young would be spending the night. Alone. In the haunted house. Well, Scout Master Matilda, or Trout, as some called her, would be there also. But still, they would be mostly alone. And frankly, Matilda was kind of a scatterbrain. But that sometimes made scout meetings even more fun. And usually gave Honey a good reason to take charge, which is something she liked to do often.

Honey worked quickly and solved all five

problems easily. She glanced at Clarice who was staring out the window. Probably daydreaming about what other trouble she could get into instead of working on math.

"Clarice," Mrs. Tenure said, "math please."

Clarice made a face and looked at her paper. Honey glanced over again. Clarice had no work done. For a moment, Honey felt bad for her—even though Clarice Kligore was famous around Sleepy Hollow Elementary for being a Class A, pain in the neck bully. It might have something to do with the fact that Clarice is the mayor's daughter. Clarice kind of believed she could get away with anything— and sometimes she did. Honey often found herself feeling sorry for her. Mostly, though, she tried to steer clear. For some reason though, today, Honey was feeling kind of friendly toward her.

But when Clarice stuck her tongue out at Honey, any feeling of tenderness toward Clarice vanished.

After a few more minutes, Mrs. Tenure asked for answers. Of course, Honey raised her hand. But Mrs. Tenure ignored her. "Noah?" Mrs. Tenure said. "Can you answer number one?"

"Yes," Noah said. "Twelve."

"Correct." Mrs. Tenure walked around the room looking at the students' papers. She stopped when she got to Clarice. "You don't have a single answer. And you haven't even tried."

Clarice stared out the window and mumbled something Honey couldn't hear.

"That's quite enough, Clarice," Mrs. Tenure said. "Perhaps you should stay after school and work on these problems."

Mrs. Tenure had obviously heard what Clarice mumbled.

"No," Clarice said. "I can't. I won't. I have something very important to do right after school."

"Then I suggest you get to work. You have ten minutes before the day is over."

Honey raised her hand. "I can help her."

"No way," Clarice said. "I'd rather have Dracula help me. Not that you're not scary enough."

Honey snorted air out her nose. She didn't mean too. It just kind of happened. And that made Clarice laugh. A few other kids laughed. Honey felt her heart break into pieces. She had to work hard to resist the urge to strike back when Clarice said, "You sound like a pig."

"Clarice Kligore!" Mrs. Tenure said. "Principal. Now!"

"Sure," Clarice said like it was nothing, like she had just been asked out to lunch at the pizza shop.

Clarice pushed her chair from her desk making it scrape across the floor. Then she stomped across the room and out the door.

"Okay," Mrs. Tenure said. "Back to math."

But the bell rang. Too late. School was over for a nice, long weekend. The weekend Honey would earn her Courage Badge.

Honey pulled her turtle-shaped backpack over her shoulders and headed straight for her best friend Becky, who was in the fifth-grade class across the hall.

"Come on," Honey said. "We have to get ready for tomorrow night!"

"Yay," Becky said. "What should we do first?"

"I don't know, but let's go to my house and make plans. We'll need to bring snacks and our flashlights, that's for sure."

Honey and Becky started down the hall. It didn't take long for Claire Sinclair to catch up. Claire and Honey were in the same class, but Honey always dashed out ahead of her to get Becky. Claire didn't mind. She usually had to organize her desk—Claire was kind of a messy student.

"Hey," Honey said.

"Hey," Claire said. "I bet that Clarice Kligore is in some pretty hot water now."

"Yeah, I'll say," Honey said. "She was really mean and snotty."

10

"What happened?" Becky asked.

Honey told Becky the story.

Becky hiked her backpack onto her shoulders. "I'm glad it was just Clarice who got into trouble. The last thing you need is an email to your mother."

"Yeah," Honey said. "She'd probably ground me from the sleepover." Honey understood the value of holding her tongue.

The girls headed across the playground. They had just reached the town green when Clarice caught up.

"Hey," Clarice called. "Thanks for getting me into trouble."

"All I did was offer to help," Honey said. "You turned it into a problem. It was your fault you were sent to the principal."

"Awww, you are such a know-it-all. Now get outta my way." Clarice barged her way past Becky and Claire. "I have more important things to do."

"Come on," Honey said. "Let's cut across

the green."

A large, black car pulled alongside the curb. Honey recognized it right away. It was Mayor Maximus Kligore's car. It was long and black and kind of scary. A broken hood ornament adorned the front. Harry told her the car was what they call a Phantom Lustro. Pretty fitting for Sleepy Hollow. The car seemed to crawl along the street, even making time slow down. As it passed, it left behind not so much exhaust but rather a frightful feeling of doom. Honey had learned to shake off the feeling for the most part, but sometimes that was difficult.

Honey hiked her turtle backpack higher onto her shoulders as Clarice opened the back door and slid inside like she was being swallowed by a whale. With the car's dark, tinted back windows Honey couldn't see Clarice anymore, and the car sped off in the opposite direction.

"Why is she so mean?" Becky asked. "She's the richest girl in town and has everything she could ever want."

12

Honey walked on a few steps. Then she stopped and said, "Maybe that's just it. Maybe having all the money and all the stuff isn't as fun as it looks."

"And that's what makes her mean?" Claire asked with a laugh. "I think she was just born that way."

"Maybe," Honey said. "But don't forget she doesn't have a mother. I guess that could make a person mean and angry." Honey walked a couple more steps. "Yeah, maybe that's it."

13

The friends shrugged and walked on toward Honey's house.

"Maybe we'll never figure it out," Honey said.

"At least we'll have three, Clarice-free days," Claire said.

"Yayyyyy," Becky said.

"I don't know," Honey said. "Maybe we can help her not be so mean."

"Maybe," Becky said. "That sounds like an impossible task—even for you."

"Uhm," Honey said. "It is a challenge. But I like challenges."

Claire groaned. "What have you got planned?"

14

Honey stopped walking. "Nothing, yet. But I'll think of something. It's hard not to feel sorry for her." Honey's backpack grew heavy.

When Turtle seemed heavier, it made Honey feel happy and safe, like a hug. Or sometimes it made her feel like she was doing the right thing and heading in the best direction. She decided that this time it meant she was on to something good.

An Impossible Race

Mrs. Wilcox, the Moon's babysitter, had just pulled a sheet of chocolate chip cookies from the oven when Honey and her friends burst through the kitchen door.

"Hey Mrs. W," Claire Sinclair said. "Looks like we're just in time."

Mrs. Wilcox laughed. "Yep, nothing like warm cookies and milk after school."

Harvest, Honey's two-year-old brother, who

was sitting in his high chair, said, "Cookie. Cookie."

Honey leaned over and gave Harvest a kiss. "Hey, bro."

Harvest clapped.

"Thank you, Mrs. Wilcox," Becky said as Mrs. Wilcox lifted cookies off the sheet and placed them gently on a pretty, blue plate.

16

"You make the best cookies in town."

"Yeah," Honey said. "You should sell them." She took a big bite. "Mrs. Wilcox's Ooey, Gooey, Best Chocolate Chip Cookies."

Mrs. Wilcox smiled. "Well, thank you, girls, but no thank you. I enjoy making cookies for the people I love. That's plenty for me."

Honey and Becky and Claire sat at the kitchen table munching cookies.

17

"So," Mrs. Wilcox said. "What have you girls got planned for the long weekend?"

The girls exchanged glances.

"Oh, we're just spending Saturday night at the old Poe house," Claire said.

"Oh dear," Mrs. Wilcox said. "Is that this weekend? Your mother did tell me. You must be very brave."

"Oh, we're not scared," Honey said. "We don't

really believe all those stories about ghosts and screams and candlesticks getting thrown across the room."

"That's good, dear," Mrs. Wilcox said. "I get the creeps when I drive past that raggedy old house. I guess I'm just an old scaredy-cat."

"Really?" Honey said. "But you take care of us. And you have to be pretty brave for that."

18

Mrs. Wilcox laughed. "That is true. You can be quite a handful, especially this little munchkin."

That was when Harvest decided to knock over his milk.

"I should have used a sippy cup," Mrs. Wilcox said.

Claire munched her cookie and then wiped chocolate from her mouth with the paper napkin Mrs. Wilcox had just given her. "I think I'll bring my baseball bat anyway—just in case I need to knock an old ghost around," she said.

"Never work," Honey said. "Your bat will go right through any ghost."

"I'm still bringing it," Claire replied.

"Now, now," said Mrs. Wilcox. "You will all be fine. I doubt you'll need that bat. People stay at the mansion quite often. It's another one of Mayor Kligore's tourist attractions." She wiped milk from Harvest's tray. "But not for me. These old bones couldn't take it."

Honey smiled into Mrs. Wilcox's eyes. "You are not old."

Mrs. Wilcox wiped Harvest's face, which was covered in chocolate. "How in the world did these tiny chocolate chips make such a mess?" she asked.

"Come on," Claire said. "Let's go to the park. We can figure out snacks and stuff there."

"You girls go on," Mrs. Wilcox said. "But be home for supper, Honey."

"I will, and oh, tell Mom I'll do my chores the minute I get home."

"Okay. Don't forget, though."

"I won't." Honey was glad that Mrs. Wilcox sometimes gave her a pass on chores.

Honey and the girls headed outside.

"Laundry," Honey said.

"What?" Claire asked.

"I have to fold laundry today. Ugh."

"Oh, don't think about it now," Becky said. "Come on, I'll race ya."

The girls took off running toward the park. "Last one to touch old Horseface is a rotten egg," Honey said.

Claire was the first to reach the huge, Headless Horseman statue in the park. She raised her arms above her head. "The winner and still champion." Reaching up on her tiptoes, she stretched her fingers to touch the

20

chin of the ferocious looking beast.

"Okay, okay," Honey said. "You're the fastest runner in Sleepy Hollow."

"Is she?" came a voice from near the Headless Horseman statue. "Is she really?"

"Clarice Kligore," Becky said. "What are you doing here?"

"Oh, nothing," Clarice said. She tucked

some stray, brown hairs behind her ears. "Just hanging out."

"Awww, c'mon," Honey replied. "You always have an angle. What is it this time?"

"Okay, okay," Clarice said. Her eyes twinkled. "How about a little challenge? Let's see who really is the fastest in Sleepy Hollow."

"What are you talking about?" Honey asked. Honey didn't trust Clarice very much.

"Just a simple race. Me against you three. I bet you two packs of Batty Bubble Gum I can reach the clock tower before any of you."

"No way," Claire said. "Everyone knows I'm the fastest runner in school."

"So don't be a chicken then. And look, I will even give you a head start."

"A head start?" Claire said. "I don't need a head start."

"Fine," Clarice said. "Let's go."

The girls lined up.

"On your mark," Becky said, "get set, GO!"

Everyone took off. Honey ran as hard as she could. She ran and ran and then looked behind her for Clarice, but she was gone. Honey ran harder and looked toward the clock tower. She could not believe her eyes. Clarice Kligore was already standing at the tower.

"That's impossible," Claire said the second her foot crossed the finish line. "You cheated."

"Now, how could I have cheated?" young Miss Kligore said. "You're batty."

"I don't know, but . . . but how did you run that fast? It's like you're the Flash." Claire bent at the waist and puffed to catch her breath.

Clarice smirked. "That's right. I'm the Flash. Now who's the fastest runner in school?"

Becky was still catching her breath. "Wow," was all she could say.

Clarice looked Honey square in the eyes.

"That'll be two packs of Batty Bubble."

"Fine, Clarice. I still think you cheated." Honey leaned against the clock tower. "But I'll get your stupid gum."

"You better," Clarice said, and she took off toward the Headless Horseman.

"How did she do that?" Honey asked. "Nobody can run that fast."

24

"I don't know," Claire said. "It was like she was running with us for a second and the next second she was at the finish line."

Honey started walking toward the swing set. "I don't know. Something isn't right. She's up to something."

"Well, if she really can run that fast," Becky said, "she should be in the Olympics."

"Yeah," Claire said. "Seriously."

"Phooey," Honey said. "I smell a rat. A big, fat rat."

MUMMY MATES
COURAGE

JUST TELL HER
TO BE NICE

"Let's change the subject," Becky said. "Who cares about Clarice Kligore? She probably found a way to cheat." She sat on the middle swing.

"Impossible," Claire said.

"All right, all right," Honey said. "I don't think we'll figure it out now. And why should we? Clarice is always up to something."

"Yeah," Becky said. "Yeah." She pumped her legs and soared high on the swing.

"I think popcorn is a must for the sleepover," Honey said changing the subject. "And we'll need cookies and juice boxes."

"Yeah," Claire said. "Trout said we should bring sandwiches because we can't use the fireplace. Too dangerous."

26

"Yeah?" Becky said. "It must be a new rule. They used to let the scouts roast hotdogs."

Honey pumped her legs harder and harder until she got the bumps. Then she waited a few seconds, and at just the exact, right moment she sailed off the swing and stuck a perfect landing on the soft grass.

Becky followed, and then Claire sailed through the air and landed the furthest away from the swings. "And I'm still the winner!" she said. "Let's see Clarice jump farther than me."

"We better head home," Honey said. "I'm

gonna give it some thought, but I think we need to add one more thing to our list."

"What?" Claire asked.

"We need to come up with a scary prank to pull on Trout."

"Oh, good idea," Claire said. "But it has to be really good. She's done this so many times she's probably been victim to every prank imaginable."

27

"Then we'll just have to think harder," Honey said.

"Maybe we'll get some ideas at the Sidewalk Sale tomorrow," Becky said.

"Sidewalk Sale. That's right. I almost forgot about it. Yeah. Let's meet in the morning, and we'll go shopping."

"Good idea," Claire said. "The Sidewalk Sale is always the best."

Becky and Claire took off toward their homes. Honey headed down Nightingale Lane toward her house.

Coming up with prank ideas was usually something Honey could do easily. Getting one over on her brother Harry was pretty simple—like opening the salt shaker too much, so it all spilled out, or substituting honey for shampoo. But this required some deep thought. Spooky pranks were not necessarily Honey's strong suit.

28

She kicked a stone. "Come on Honey Moon, think."

That was when she saw Clarice Kligore again.

"Aww, c'mon Clarice," Honey said. "What gives?"

"I'll tell you what gives. You are gonna give me my gum."

29

"I don't have it yet. I'll get it tomorrow."

Honey tried to walk around Clarice. But Clarice wouldn't let her.

"Now. I want it now."

"I said I don't have it yet, and I have to get home for supper." She tried again to step around Clarice. But again Clarice stopped her—this time she tripped Honey, and she fell on her knees. Honey felt pain race through her body. But she refused to cry. Instead, she pulled herself up and got face-to-face with Clarice.

"Why are you such a bully? Leave me alone." Honey tried to walk away.

"I'll expect my gum in the morning," Clarice said. "Don't forget."

Honey kept walking. "Yeah, yeah," she said. "Tomorrow. You'll get your precious gum tomorrow." Honey walked a few more steps. Her knees stung, but she didn't want to let Clarice know that they hurt. She waited until Clarice was out of sight before she started to limp a little.

Mary Moon was home when Honey got there. And that's when she turned on the waterworks—well at least a little.

"Sit down and tell me what happened," Honey's mom said.

Honey rolled up her pants and exposed two mildly scraped knees.

"Clarice Kligore blocked my path and then knocked me ·down."

Mary Moon dabbed at Honey's knees with a wet paper towel. "This isn't too bad. Just a typical road rash. You don't even need a Band-Aid."

"But it hurts, Mom."

"The pain will be gone by supper," Mary said. "And next time, if you see Clarice, cross the street or walk the other way."

"It's not that easy."

31

"Bully-type people like Clarice can be difficult," Honey's mom said as she rolled Honey's pant legs down. "But it's best not to engage her. Just ignore her. And if I have to, I'll call the school again."

"Are you sure I don't need a Band-Aid?"

Mary Moon shook her head. One thing about having a nurse for a mom is that you can't argue the medical stuff or fake it either. "Okay, now get washed up for supper. Spaghetti and meatballs."

"Great," Honey said.

Honey set off toward the powder room.

"Oh, Honey," Mary called. "Don't forget the laundry."

Ugh. "But my knees. They hurt so much. Maybe Harry should do it."

Honey waited for her mom's reply. It never came. So after washing her hands, Honey went to the laundry room. She hauled the basket of towels and shirts and jeans into the living room. "At least it's not Harry's icky boxers."

Harry came bounding down the stairs like he was being chased by a swarm of bees. "Mooooooommmmm," he called. "I need my blue t-shirt. The one with the magic top hat."

Honey spied the shirt in the basket. She grabbed it and crammed it behind her back.

"In the laundry," Mary said. "Should be with Honey."

"Can I have my shirt, please," Harry asked Honey.

"Oh, gee," she said as she looked through the basket. "I don't see it."

"What?" Harry said. "Mom said you had it. Now give it to me."

Honey looked again. "Sorry, dear *brothere*, but as you can see the shirt is not here."

"Mooommm," Harry called. "Honey doesn't have it."

Mary Moon came out of the kitchen wiping her hands on a small, yellow towel. "Really, I'm sure I saw it."

Honey laughed. "You really are a great magician. You can even make your shirts disappear."

Harry screwed up his face. "Ahhhh, I get it. You have it. You're hiding my shirt."

"I am not. And if you are so good at magic

you should be able to make it reappear. So go ahead, Harry, say the word."

Harry shook his head. "Okay, I'll play along. Abracadabra."

Honey said, "Nope. Not good enough. Louder. So the shirt can hear."

"ABRACADABRA!" Harry shouted so loud that Half Moon, the dog, barked.

Honey pulled the shirt from behind her back. "Presto. Great trick."

Harry snatched the shirt from Honey's hand. "Very funny."

"Awww c'mon, Harry," Mary said. "She was just playing around."

"But she's making me late. The Good Mischief Team has a meeting tonight, unlike you and your laundry."

Honey folded one of Harvest's shirts and placed it in a pile. "Well, it just so happens that

34

I do have something going on. I am getting ready to spend the night at the Poe House."

Harry nearly doubled-over he laughed so hard. "That place? It's not so scary—except for, well, you'll find out."

"Except for what?" Honey asked.

"Let's just say the Headless Horseman gets a little restless on scout sleepover nights." Then he shuddered.

35

Honey grabbed a pair of Harry's jeans and threw them at him. "Don't scare me."

"Oh, great," Harry said. "I'll wear these."

"Ugh. Go to your stupid meeting."

Harry didn't say a word. Well, he laughed a little and headed upstairs.

"Mom," Honey said. "Why do you let him belittle me like that?"

"Oh, Honey. You kind of started it. And

36

besides, he's just kidding."

Honey took a deep breath and folded the last shirt in her basket. "I guess. And I guess it's okay because I know Harry doesn't mean the things he says to me, but you know Mom—"

"What's that?"

"Making fun or belittling someone is not always funny."

Mary Moon helped Honey place the folded laundry into the basket. "I know, dear. Did something happen?"

"Aww, it was nothing, really." Honey placed another folded shirt onto the growing pile. "Just that nasty Clarice Kligore, again. She called me scary, like Dracula. Am I scary? And well, you already know she tripped me and made me skin my knees."

"Of course not," Mary said. "Clarice is just, well she's just mean because she's so insecure. It's hard growing up without a mother."

31

"Yeah, I guess so."

"But you're right, Honey. Bullying is never okay. Maybe you could find a way to help the situation."

"Yeah? That was kind of what I was thinking today, but after she said I was scarier than Dracula and tripped me, I kind of lost the urge to help her."

Mary patted Honey's shoulder. "I know. But I am proud of you for not retaliating. And sometimes doing the right thing even when you don't want to can be a very good thing."

"Thanks, Mom."

Mary Moon picked up the basket. "You relax. I'll carry this upstairs."

That night, Honey had a hard time falling asleep and not only because of the sometimes mournful cries that filtered through the Sleepy Hollow air. She kept thinking about Clarice and bullying and the Poe Mansion and the Sidewalk Sale and pretty much everything in the world. Some nights were like that, but this night Honey couldn't shake the feeling she was supposed to do something to help Clarice even after what she did.

She looked over at her turtle backpack. It hung from her desk chair. Turtle's googly eyes looked straight at her as a shaft of light from the street lamp broke through the curtains.

"Well," Honey said. "Do you have any bright ideas?"

Honey waited, but Turtle didn't say a word. She rolled over and closed her eyes, and that was when she was hit by blinding inspiration. "Maybe I can help Clarice feel better about herself and then she won't need to pick on me or anyone else."

She sat straight up. She looked at Turtle. "My Courage Badge could have a double meaning. One for spending the night in a haunted house and the other for helping Clarice find her niceness. Maybe someone just needs to tell her it's okay to be nice."

39

40

TWO PACKS OF GUM

Saturday mornings were always the best. Honey could sleep late and her mom or dad usually made a special breakfast. And this morning was no different. Today, Mary Moon made strawberry-stuffed French toast to celebrate the long weekend.

Honey sat at the table. Harry was already gobbling down his share, and Harvest was elbow deep in strawberries and whipped cream.

"Thanks, Mom," Honey said. "My favorite."

"You're welcome, Honey. Enjoy." Mary set a plate brimming with the ooey, gooey, delectable breakfast in front of Honey.

"What? No powdered sugar?" Honey asked.

"But Honey, look at all that whipped cream," her mom said. "It's like Mount Everest on a plate."

42

"Aww, come on. Just a little, around the edges," Honey replied. "It will make it look like it's still snowing on Mt. Everest."

"You know," Harry said. "You should write some of this stuff down."

Honey looked at Harry. She wasn't quite sure if he was serious or poking fun at her again. She chose the former.

"Why, thank you, Harry Moon. I think I will enter it my journal and not only that," she pulled her cell from her pocket, "I am going to snap a shot on account of this breakfast being the most beautiful breakfast ever."

43

"Thank you, Honey," Mary Moon said. She was standing at the kitchen counter eating her French toast. That was when Honey noticed her mom was wearing her turquoise scrubs.

"You have a shift today?" Honey asked.

"Yeah. I'm filling in. Could be a long day."

"Okay," Honey said. "Will you be home before I leave for the haunted house?"

"I should be. But if not, Dad will be here. He'll drive you."

Honey looked at her plate. She really wanted her mom to drive. Even though she was acting brave, Honey was a little nervous about the haunted house, and her mom was better at keeping Honey calm than her dad.

44

"Don't worry," Mary Moon said. "You will do fine. But Honey, if you wouldn't mind, throw a load of towels into the washer this morning. And Harry, that yard could use some attention, don't forget the trash, and please, clean your room. It's a disaster area."

"Okay, okay," they said.

"Where is Dad?" Harry asked. "I can't believe he's passing up strawberry French toast."

"Auto parts store. He'll be home soon. And he already had his share—twice."

Honey concentrated on her breakfast. She loved strawberries and whipped cream. It was like heaven, sweet and comforting. "Are you sure he'll be home soon, Mom? Dad at the auto parts store is like Harry at the Magic Shoppe. They both kind of get lost and hypnotized in those places."

Mary Moon smiled. "Yes, I know. But, he knows I have to work."

"It's too bad," Honey said. "You're going to miss the Sidewalk Sale."

"I know," Mary replied as she sipped coffee. "I bet there will be some great buys."

"I'm hoping to find some things for tonight," Honey said. "I'm meeting Becky and Claire soon."

"You might want to grab some rubber spiders," Mary said.

Harry laughed. "Rubber spiders. Totally amateur."

"Maybe you should get started on the lawn," Mary Moon replied.

"Yeah, yeah, okay," he said.

Honey licked the last of the strawberries from her plate. "Thanks, Mom, you really make the best stuffed French toast."

"Thank you." Her mom glanced at the clock. "Oh dear, I have to leave, and your father isn't home yet."

46

"Told you so," Honey said. But when she saw the sour look on her mom's face she quickly added, "But no problem, I'm here, and Harry is in the back yard. I can watch Harvest."

Her mom grabbed her bag from the kitchen counter. "Uhm, okay. I'm sure Dad will be home any minute."

Honey pulled a strawberry from Harvest's hair. "Go, Mom. We'll be fine."

"Okay," Mary Moon said. "You're the best.

Text me if you need me. And Honey, in case I don't see you before you leave for the sleepover, remember, it's really not haunted. Nothing bad will happen to you or anyone else. It's all in fun—the Sleepy Hollow way."

"Thanks, Mom." Honey pulled another piece of strawberry from Harvest's hair.

Mary Moon dashed out the kitchen door and headed for the garage.

47

"Gee," Honey said, "Mom must think I really am growing up." She lifted Harvest out of his high chair. "Come on. Let's go play with blocks until Daddy gets home."

"Blocks," Harvest said.

Honey thought Harvest had a future in architecture as she watched him construct a tall tower. Too bad it didn't stand tall for long. Half Moon bounded into the room wagging his tail so hard he knocked the block tower over. Harvest cried.

"Oh, it's okay," Honey said. "We can rebuild it even better."

Honey heard a noise in the kitchen. It startled her at first but then she figured it was just her dad coming home.

"Dad?" Honey called. "Is that you?"

"Only me," John Moon called.

48

"Okay," Honey said. "Gee, Harvest. If Dad coming home is enough to scare me how will I survive tonight?"

"Hey, Dad," Honey said. "I was just watching Harvest until you got home. But now I gotta go."

"Where to?" John asked when he entered the living room.

"I'm meeting Becky at the green. Then we're going over to Shopper's Row. Today's the Annual Spooky Spring Sidewalk Sale."

"Now that's a mouthful." John Moon picked Harvest up. "How's my little man?"

Harvest giggled.

"So can I go?" Honey asked. "I have my own money."

"Did you finish your chores?"

Ugh. "Not yet. I was busy watching Harvest after Mom left for the hospital."

49

John nodded. "Okay, I'll let it slide since you were babysitting. Go on. But check in with me later."

"Right," Honey said.

Honey ran upstairs and into her room. She grabbed her backpack. "Come on," she said. "You're with me." She slung the backpack over her shoulders.

"See ya," she called to anyone who was listening and ran out the front door.

Becky was already waiting at the green.

"Hey," Honey called. "Sorry, I'm late. I had to watch Harvest until my dad got home."

"No problem," Becky said.

"Let's go swing," Honey said. "The Sidewalk Sale isn't open yet."

"Yeah, okay. Hey, have you seen Claire?"

50

"Not yet. But I'm sure she'll show up."

Honey and Becky got to the swings, but one of the swings was already occupied. By Clarice.

"Good morning, nerds," Clarice said. "Where's the gum you owe me?"

Honey snorted air out her nose. "Oh come on, Clarice, the stores aren't even open yet. You'll get your gum."

"Two packs," Clarice said. "Batty Bubble."

"I know," Honey said.

Clarice jumped off the swing. "I gotta go. How 'bout we meet near the candy shop in one hour."

"Great," Honey said in a way that made it sound like it wasn't really great—merely tolerable. "See you there."

Clarice smirked. "Two packs."

"Geeze," Becky said. "How many times are you gonna say it. We know. Two packs."

Clarice smirked again and took off toward Shopper's Row.

"She is such a pain," Honey said as she pumped her legs. "Mom says it's on account of her not having a mom."

"Claire's parents are divorced, and she's not mean."

"Yeah, but it's not the same. No one knows what happened to Clarice's mom. I don't think she ever sees her."

"Claire sees her mom sometimes."

Honey swung faster. "But maybe if she was nicer, more people would like her, and well, it could help. I'm gonna try and get her to at least try to be nice."

Becky pumped her legs a few times and then said, "I don't know. She's always got friends."

52

"Well, I still want to try and help her see that being a bully isn't the best thing."

Becky jumped from the highest point possible on the swings. Honey followed her. She flapped her arms three times before sticking a perfect landing. "Nailed it."

"Seriously?" Becky said. "But how on earth can you convince Clarice Kligore to be nice? I think it's in her DNA to be mean."

53

Honey shrugged. "Don't know yet. And I've been thinking, we need candy for tonight. And rubber spiders."

"Lots of them," Becky said. "And lots of candy."

Finally, Claire showed up. She was wearing her baseball cap, as usual.

"Hey guys," she said. "I overslept."

"It's okay," Honey said. "We were just on our way to the Sidewalk Sale."

"To get Clarice's gum?" Claire said with a smirk.

"Yeah," Honey said. "And some stuff for tonight."

Shopper's Row was already a busy place. Even though it was early April, the street looked like autumn with fallen leaves and pumpkins lining the street. Hay bales and scarecrows decorated many of the shops. The nutty, rich aroma of pumpkin and nutmeg wafted through the air. Honey took a deep breath. "As weird as it is," she said, "I will never get tired of that smell." It was one of the only things she truly enjoyed about Sleepy Hollow.

Some of the stores weren't even open yet, but people were doing some window-shopping. Most of the store owners and clerks were setting their products out on the sidewalk getting ready for the big day. The Phantom Produce storeowner, Brice Larson, was setting out barrels of apples and boxes of squash and tomatoes.

54

"Oh, apples," Honey said, "we should bring apples. We can have an apple dunking contest."

"Maybe we can make caramel apples," Becky said.

"Good idea. We can make those easy before it's time to go to the Poe house," Honey said.

A young woman was setting out creams and lotions and pretty smelling soaps. "I don't think we'll need tiny soap for tonight," Claire said.

"Is the Screaming Jelly Bean open yet?' Honey asked. "We'll need a package of caramels, lots of extra candy, and, of course, Clarice's gum."

Becky shrugged. "Don't know. Let's check."

"Look," Claire called. "It's open, and Mrs. Slaughter is setting candy out on those tables. Yum. I want some Sour Squid."

55

"Well, I have to get two packs of Batty Bubble and caramels for the apples first. Then I can stock up on my favorite candy—Malted Milk Mummies."

The candy shop had just opened, and Honey didn't even need to go inside to buy the gum or the caramels or even the Malted Mummies. She bought it all right there on the sidewalk. "Thank you," she said as the clerk dropped change into Honey's hand.

56

"Have a Spooky good day," the clerk replied.

Honey groaned. "Now I just have to find that pest Clarice."

"Look," Becky said. "There she is. Over at the rock and mineral display."

"Now why would she be interested in rocks?" Honey said.

"Maybe 'cause she has them in her head," Claire said.

Honey took a deep breath. "Okay, I know it was just a joke, but I think we need to be more careful about our jokes. People still get hurt. Even Clarice."

Claire Sinclair wrinkled her face at Becky. "What's with her?"

"She's kind of made Clarice her new project. She wants to make her nice."

Claire laughed so hard her cap fell off. "That's like trying to make a porcupine into a teddy bear."

Honey walked up to Clarice. "Here. Two packs of Batty Bubble. Now we're square."

"Thanks," Clarice said. She crammed the gum into her pocket. "Have fun tonight. But I'd watch my step if I were you. That place is pretty scary."

"Thanks for the advice," Honey said. "Have you ever thought about joining Mummy Mates?"

Clarice busted out laughing. "Me? A scout? Too lame for me."

Clarice walked away toward the green.

"Okay," Honey said. "I tried."

Becky popped a piece of candy into her mouth. "What do you suppose she meant by that?"

58

"By what?" Honey asked.

"About watching our step," Becky said.

Honey just shook her head and started down Shopper's Row. But she had only taken two steps when she was suddenly stopped by Clarice.

"Clarice!" Honey said. "I just saw you. And you were going the opposite way."

Clarice let out a snort. "You did not. I've been right here the whole time—waiting for you. Now hand over my gum."

"But she just gave it to you," Becky said.

"Yeah," Claire said. "Like a minute ago."

"No, you didn't. Now pay up."

Honey didn't say anything for a moment. She stood there staring down Clarice until finally she said, "Something's not right. I just saw you over there." She pointed behind her. "I gave you the gum, and you walked away toward the green. There is no way you could be standing right here. Even you are not that fast."

59

Clarice shrugged. "But I am standing here. Now give me the gum."

"No," Honey said. "I already paid the bet. You have some kind of trick going on."

And that was when Harry happened by. He lifted his chin at Clarice. "Hey."

"It's okay, Harry," Honey said. "I can handle this."

"So pay up," Clarice said.

"No. I told you, I already gave it to you. You're just trying to get paid twice."

Harry stepped between Honey and Clarice. "Maybe you should just go, Clarice," he said.

"Yeah, yeah," Clarice said. "It's too bad you need your big brother to fight your battles. I'll see ya around."

60

Honey watched Clarice run off toward the green. This time Honey kept her eye on her until she was out of sight.

"Honestly, Harry," Honey said. "I gave her the gum."

"I believe you," Harry said. "She's just trying to get it out of you twice."

"She's so mean," Becky said.

"But really," Claire said. "How did she get to that spot so quickly? It's like the race yesterday.

Something is definitely weird."

"Listen," Harry said. "I'm meeting Hao and Bailey. I have to go."

"Thanks," Honey said.

Harry smiled. "No problem. And say, be careful tonight. Could be some scary moments at the mansion."

Claire laughed. "Awww, c'mon, it's all fake stuff. They would never let a group of girls sleepover in a truly haunted, haunted mansion."

Harry shrugged. "Maybe. But we do live in Sleepy Hollow."

"Come on. We'll be fine." Honey grabbed Becky's hand. "Trout will be with us."

"That's what I'm afraid of," Claire replied.

62

SHOPPER'S ROW

The wind started to pick up as gray clouds rolled overhead. This was not unusual for Sleepy Hollow, where every day is Halloween night.

"I hope it doesn't rain," Honey said as she and her friends walked down Shopper's Row.

"Yeah, me too," Becky said.

"Not me," Claire said. "I hope it rains and even thunders tonight, and I hope there's lightning too. Perfect for a haunted house."

Becky grabbed Honey's hand. "Now I'm getting scared."

"Oh don't be," Honey said. "We're perfectly safe. Nothing will happen. It's all in your head."

"But what if there really is a ghost?"

"No such thing," Claire said.

Honey walked on a few steps and then stopped. "Uhm, but I have a sneaky feeling we just might see a ghost tonight."

More and more people gathered on Shopper's Row. The stores had, by now, set out their wares and goodies. There were wind chimes of flying bats and ghosts and dream catchers and even nightmare makers hanging from displays. Claire stopped and pointed out one of the dream catchers. "Look at this one. It has a skeleton woven into it. Who wants to dream about skeletons?"

"Not me," Honey said.

Another gust of wind blew past causing

a small, fallen-leaf tornado near Honey. The wind chimes jingled with a kind of eerie, Sleepy Hollow sound.

Honey knew that Harry sometimes felt the wind when Rabbit was nearby. She pulled Turtle from her shoulders and looked him square in his googly eyes. "Are you trying to get my attention?"

Claire practically fell on the ground she laughed so hard.

65

"Wow, Honey," Becky said. "It's one thing to talk to your backpack when it's just us, but not in a crowd. It makes you look like a baby."

Honey felt like Becky had just punched her in the stomach. A baby? "Sorry," Honey said. "It's just that the wind—"

"It's just wind," Claire said. "This is Sleepy Hollow where every day is Halloween night. Gotta expect some wind and dark clouds."

"You're right," Honey said. She slipped Turtle onto her back. "Let's go to your house. We have work to do."

"Don't look now," Becky said. "But there's Clarice over there."

"Where?" Honey asked.

"Near the bakery."

"Oh, I see her," Honey said.

"Maybe we should steer clear," Claire said. "Who knows what she's up to."

66

Honey squeezed past a few people who stopped to purchase Paralyzed Pimple Pretzels with Cheddar Scream dipping sauce. "Let's go see. Maybe she's just hanging around and being normal."

"Aww let's just go to the general store and buy things we need for tonight," Becky said.

"No," Honey said. "I want to keep an eye on her."

Just as they reached the bakery, Clarice walked out of the shop.

Honey stopped dead in her tracks. "Hold

on, that's impossible. Clarice is standing near that street light."

"But she also came out of the bakery," Becky said.

"There's two?" Claire said. "How is that even possible?"

"I don't know, but I'm gonna find out." Honey marched toward the two Clarices.

"What gives?" Honey said. "There are two of you?"

Clarice number one nearly choked. "Oh, hey."

"Yeah, spill it, Clarice," Becky said. "You have a twin?"

"All right, all right. So you caught us," Clarice said. She motioned for the other Clarice to join her. "This is my cousin, Bella."

68

"But you're identical," Becky said. "I didn't know cousins could be identical."

Bella smiled. "It's pretty rare, but here we are."

Honey looked at Clarice and then at Bella. She looked back at Clarice and then again at Bella. "This is surreal—even for Sleepy Hollow. Since when are you twins? I've known you our whole lives."

She walked around them. They not only shared the same face with the same pointy nose and shifty eyes but they were wearing the same clothes—a striped shirt, jeans, and pink sneakers. Their hair was done exactly the same also.

"So that's how you won the race," Honey said. "You and your cousin cheated. She was already waiting at the finish line."

Clarice smirked, but Bella looked at her shoes.

"And that's how you tried to tell Honey she never gave you the gum—you thought you could get paid twice," Claire said.

69

Honey noticed that Bella still could not look her or Claire in the face.

"Pretty cool, isn't it?" Clarice said.

"No," Honey said. "It's not cool when you cheat people."

Clarice started to walk away, but Honey stopped her. "So how come we never met Bella before?"

"Yeah, that's right," Becky said. "Where've

you been hiding her?"

"Nowhere," Clarice. "She lives in Philadelphia, and this is the first time she's visited. We play tricks all the time when I visit her in Philly though."

Honey had a hard time taking her eyes off Bella. She was beginning to think that Bella was less than a willing participant in Clarice's games.

70

There they stood, side-by-side, Clarice and Bella as similar as two peas in a pod or two bats in a belfry. But maybe they were only the same on the outside. At least Honey hoped so. One Clarice was tough enough. But two? That could be impossible.

"It really is amazing," Becky said.

"Pretty sweet, huh," Clarice said.

"Say," Becky said, "I heard that twins have mental connections—you know they can read each other's minds. Can you guys do that?"

Finally, Bella perked up a little. Clarice and

Bella looked at each other. "Sure," they said at the same time. "Try us."

"Wait," Honey said. "This isn't the time for games. Clarice cheated us."

Claire smiled. "Aww, so what? It's kind of funny, now."

Honey remembered her mission—trying to make Clarice nicer. And what better way than to be nice to her also? Now that the secret was out it really didn't seem all that bad anymore.

"Okay," Honey said. "Bella, tell me a state capital, and we'll see if Clarice can name it."

Bella pulled a small notebook and pen from her pocket. She motioned for Honey to follow her. Then Bella wrote "Boise" in the notebook.

"Okay," Honey said. "There is no way Clarice could have seen that. So tell me, what state capital did she choose?"

Claire stared long and hard at Bella. Then

she said, "Boise."

Honey held up the page for the others to see.

"Wowzers," Becky said. "That's incredible."

"Do it again," Claire Sinclair said. "But this time use baseball teams."

"Uhm," Bella said. "That's a little tougher. But okay."

Clarice looked square at Bella again and said, "Baseball team."

Once again Honey and Bella walked away and turned their backs. Bella wrote on a piece of notebook paper.

"Okay," Honey said. "You will never guess this one."

Clarice looked at Bella with squinty eyes like she was trying to read her mind. "Cleveland Indians," she said.

"That's impossible," Honey said. "It's a trick.

12

73

It has to be."

Bella shrugged. Claire shrugged.

"Come on, Bella. Let's go get a Frankenweiner." Clarice said as she grabbed Claire's baseball cap and yanked it off her head.

"Hey," Claire said. "Give it back."

But Clarice and Bella ran down the street laughing. At least Honey was certain Clarice was laughing.

"This has to stop," Honey said. "She can't keep doing this stuff. Even when we're nice to her, she still acts mean."

"And now she has Bella to help her," Becky said. "It's like an impossible team to defeat."

"Well, I'm not letting them get away." Claire took off running after them. "Stop. Thief," she called. "Stop them. They stole my hat."

Honey dashed after Claire. Becky dashed after Honey. All three of them stopped as Officer Ortiz stepped out in front of Clarice.

"She took my hat," Claire said.

"Aww, don't be such a crybaby," Clarice said.

Officer Ortiz put out his hand, and Clarice gave him Claire's hat. "See if I care," she said. "It's a dumb hat anyway. You're such a weirdo."

"Cut it out, Miss Kligore," Officer Ortiz said. "Or I'll have to tell your father."

"Fat lotta good that will do," Honey said. "She gets away with everything in this town."

"Now, now, Honey," Officer Ortiz said, "you've had your share of . . . shall we say mishaps? This isn't so bad."

"I suppose," Honey said.

That was when Office Ortiz scratched his chin. He pointed at Clarice and then at Bella. "Hold on a second. There's two of you?"

15

Clarice laughed. "Yep. Two of me."

Bella looked away again.

"Well," Officer Ortiz said, "you behave yourself, both of you."

"I'm leaving," Claire said.

Honey and Becky followed Claire down the street.

Honey readjusted her backpack. It had loosened up at she was running. It wasn't easy to run with a backpack filled with apples and caramels.

"Come on," Becky said. "Let's go to my house and get ready for tonight."

"Yeah," Honey said. "We have some pranks to plan."

"Pranks?" Claire said. "Who we gonna prank? Each other?"

"No, silly," Honey said. "Trout, of course."

76

After they had walked a few minutes, Honey stopped. "You know," she said, "I've been thinking. I bet that Clarice and her cousin are gonna pull something at the mansion tonight."

"You think?" Becky said. "But they aren't part of the Mummy Mates."

"Doesn't matter. They'll sneak inside. We just have to be ready for them."

CRAFTS AND COOKIES

Honey loved going to Becky's house. It was without a doubt the prettiest, and maybe even the silliest, house in town. Her parents were artists and made crafts and pottery and things. Honey especially loved the handmade whirligigs in the front yard. Her favorites were the funny goose with the wings that spun in circles whenever the wind blew and the old man milking a cow. Becky's mother hand-crafted them in their garage. Of course, there were also whirligigs of vampires and bats and even a werewolf. It was Sleepy Hollow, after all.

"Come on," Becky said, "let's go to the craft room. We can work there."

"Sounds good," Honey said.

"Hey, Mom," Becky called. "Honey and Claire are here. We're gonna work in the craft room."

78

Mrs. Young walked out of the kitchen. "That's fine. I was making some candles."

"Ooooo, candles," Honey said. "We could use candles tonight."

Mrs. Young laughed. "Uhm, I don't think so. Too dangerous in an old house like that. Flashlights will have to do."

"Okay, I guess so," Honey said. "But Mrs. Young, can you help us make caramel apples?"

"Now that's a good idea," Mrs. Young said.

Becky's craft room was quite a spectacular place. The walls were lined with cabinets chock-full of everything an artist could want, from watercolor paints to wallpaper scraps to yarn and glue. Honey didn't even know there were so many different types of glue in the world.

"But we really don't need to make crafts, today," Honey said. "We need to plan ahead in case Clarice and her cousin decide to crash the sleepover. And of course, we need

something to prank Trout."

Claire climbed up onto one of the stools near the craft table. "I think Trout will be easy to get. We could probably just dangle a big, rubber spider in front of her, and she'd scream her lungs out."

Honey laughed. "Yeah, you're right. We really need to be ready for Clarice and her cousin. Don't forget we have two Clarices now."

"Double trouble," Claire said.

"I hate to admit this," Becky said as she sat on the other stool, "but I'm a little scared."

"Of Clarice?" Honey said. "What can she do besides scare us?"

"Or try to?" Claire fidgeted with a roll of ribbon. "We just need to be expecting it."

"Yeah, the trick is to not let her surprise us," Honey said.

"No," Becky said. "I'm scared of the real thing. I mean what if that old house really is haunted?"

Claire laughed. "Don't be silly. It's just a big, empty, old house with cobwebs and loose boards and junk."

"I hope you're right," Becky said. "I'll do my best not to be scared."

Honey looked into Becky's eyes. She could tell that Becky was truly frightened about the possibilities. And even though Claire was not exactly acting like a bully, Honey thought it might have been a little unfair of Claire not to take Becky's fear seriously.

"It's okay, Becky," Honey said. "Look, if you get scared just tell us. We'll take good care of you and make sure you are never alone. Being scared is your honest feeling, and there's nothing wrong with that."

Becky smiled. "Thank you."

Honey glared at Claire who said, "Oh, yeah, right. We'll protect you."

Honey grabbed a piece of cardboard that was on the table. "Look, I think if we cut out the shape of a ghost in this cardboard, we can shine a flashlight and project it on a wall."

"Oh yeah, we can," Becky said. "I can cut spiders too."

"Great idea," Claire said. "Then we can shine it on the wall and scare the bejeebers out of Trout."

"Right," Honey said. "That's the kind of stuff we need."

They continued coming up with more pranks and cutting out ghosts and spiders for a little while. But soon it was time to make the caramel apples.

It didn't take long for Mrs. Young to melt the caramels. Honey thought it actually took longer for them to unwrap each one.

"Shoulda bought the unwrapped ones," Honey said.

"Nah," Mrs. Young said. "These are cheaper."

Honey stuck one of the pointy sticks through an onion.

"Is that an onion?" Mrs. Young said.

"Yep," Honey said. "That's the big prank."

83

Mrs. Young laughed. "Oh, I get it. And who is the prank-ee?"

"Scout Master Matilda," Becky said.

"Are you sure you want to do that?" Mrs. Young said. "She might get pretty upset."

"Nah, Trout's a good sport," Honey said dipping an apple into the luscious, golden caramel. "And I wouldn't doubt it if Trout has a few scary pranks up her sleeve, too."

"Oh, I see," Mrs. Young said. "Just be careful.

DOUBLE TROUBLE

Don't let things get out of hand."

"We won't, Mom," Becky sad. "We just want to be ready for anything."

"And we are going to be prepared," Claire said.

Mrs. Young smiled. "Well, a scout is always prepared."

84

"Thanks, Mom," Becky said. "This is gonna be so much fun."

"Sounds like it," Mrs. Young said. "But be on guard. I hear that place can be pretty scary. It was when I did that Courage Challenge."

"You?" Honey said as she dipped the onion into the pot of melted caramel.

"Sure. Nearly everyone in town has done it. Kind of a right of passage around here. But once you've done it, you're kind of sworn to secrecy about what really goes on."

"Secrecy?" Honey said. "How come?"

"Well, you know, that way it stays just as mysterious and haunting for the next group of kids. Best way to keep the fright alive."

Honey put her hand on her knee because it was shaking. "So there really are creepy things?"

"Maybe," Mrs. Young said as she rolled one of the caramel apples in crushed pecans. "Maybe not."

85

"Now I'm scared again," Becky said.

"Oh, I'm sorry, sweetie," Mrs. Young said. "I'm sure you'll be fine. You all will."

Honey swallowed. "Sure," she said with a shaky voice. "We'll be f-f-fine."

They finished the apples, which Mrs. Young wrapped in wax paper and placed in a large plastic container. "Now don't forget which one is the onion."

"We won't," said Honey. "I wrapped a black string around the stick."

"Good idea," Mrs. Young said.

Honey crammed some cookies into her backpack. Then she and Claire walked home together. They made plans to meet Becky at the old Poe house at six o'clock. Claire took off down her street. "See you at six."

Honey had just gotten to the Headless Horseman when Clarice jumped out and yelled, "Boo."

"Oh, come on Clarice you are going to have to do better than that."

"Really," Clarice said. "I guess you're right."

And then all of a sudden Honey jumped three feet off the ground because she felt something on her shoulder. She turned quickly and there stood Bella, smiling.

"You mean like that?" Clarice said.

"Very funny," Honey said. Her heart was beating out of her chest. "Very funny."

"We thought so," Bella said.

Honey had jumped so hard that Turtle fell off her shoulders. She bent down to pick him up when Clarice said, "When are you going to outgrow that silly turtle. It's for babies."

"Ha," Honey said. "Fat lot of good you know. This is no ordinary Turtle."

Bella looked at Honey. "What do you mean?"

But Honey didn't have a chance to answer.

Clarice grabbed Bella's hand. "Let's go."

Geeze. It was like they were warming up for tonight. Honey knew she had to be extra prepared for their antics.

"Thanks for defending me," Turtle said.

Honey walked toward home, this time making sure to look behind every bush—just in case Clarice had something else planned.

When she got home, she threw open the front door. "I'm gonna get her."

"Get who?" John Moon asked. He was sitting with Harvest on the living room floor.

"Clarice Kligore. She keeps . . . bothering me."

"Oh, well you know what I always say."

"Yeah, yeah. Turn the other cheek and all that but, Dad, I think this requires a little something more."

"Like what?"

"I'm not sure, yet. But something."

John Moon sat Harvest on the couch. "Now

listen, Honey. You be careful. I don't want you to get into trouble. This Courage Challenge is a Mummy Scouts event. Keep it that way. No personal vendettas."

Honey folded her arms across her chest. "But Dad, Clarice and her cousin are planning something tonight."

"Okay, I wouldn't doubt it. But tell Scout Master Matilda and let her help you deal with it."

"But Dad, Trout is just so . . . so scatter-brained sometimes."

"So? She's still the scout master, and you should really let her in on anything you might have planned. For safety reasons, mostly."

"Okay, okay," Honey said. "I just want to be ready for her and her cousin."

"Cousin?"

"Yeah," Honey said. She tickled Harvest.

"Clarice has an identical cousin, Bella. They're like twins. They've been pulling pranks all over town. I'm sure I'm not their only target."

"Wow," John Moon said. "That's really odd. But, even still, you be careful and tell Trout about your plans. Or, better yet, maybe I can call the mayor's office—"

"Jumpin' tiddlywinks!" Honey said. "This is getting ridiculous. No, Dad. I'm not a baby."

90

"Okay, okay," John said. "Just trying to help."

Honey shook her head. "I'm gonna go get my gear ready for tonight. I am not scared."

THE OLD POE HOUSE

The old Poe house sat like a big, clunky turkey on the edge of town. It was big, gray, and three floors tall with porches on the first and second floors. There were so many windows it was hard to count, and there were dozens of shutters, some still hinged while others were hanging off or broken or gone.

The house had three dormers on the third floor that made Honey think of wizard's hats and odd occurrences that can only take place in an attic. Giant, gnarled, old oak trees surrounded the house on all sides, and some were as dead as the house. Others stood, for some inexplicable but very Sleepy Hollow reason, in a state of perpetual autumn with orange and red leaves blazing against the bright, blue New England sky.

Honey's father opened the side van door and helped Honey with her gear—a sleeping bag, a pillow, and, of course, her turtle backpack.

9292

Honey grabbed Turtle and quickly shrugged him onto her shoulders. There was something always comforting about the backpack, and although she wouldn't say it out loud, standing there looking at the scary old relic made Honey a little nervous. She was glad Turtle was with her. She really didn't care what Clarice or Bella or anyone thought.

The wind kicked up and leaves swirled around Honey's feet.

"Where are the other scouts?" John Moon asked.

"Oh, they'll be here. I think we're a little early. But it looks like Trout is here. That's her car." Honey pointed to a bright yellow Volkswagen Beetle.

"Okay, do you want to go inside?"

Honey looked at the house and a chill wriggled down her spine. "Uhm, no, let's wait for Becky and Claire."

"Is that all who are coming?" Mr. Moon set Honey's sleeping bag on top of the car.

93

"Yes," Honey said. "We were the only ones brave enough to take the challenge. We all really, really want our Courage Badges."

Honey looked at the creepy, old house. "Do you think we'll get cell service in there?"

"Sure," Dad said. "At least, I think so. You're not that far out of town. But you never know." Then he smiled and winked. "Who knows what kind of ghostly interference there might be."

"Oh, Dad, there's no such thing as ghosts."

A car pulled up. It was Mrs. Young with Becky, and she was quickly followed by Claire's dad in his blue sports car. He had the top down even though there was a bit of chill in the air. Claire waved.

"Oh, good," Honey said. "Claire's here."

"Yeah," Honey's dad said. "I love that car."

The three girls stood with their parents and waited for Scout Master Matilda.

94

"It's bigger than I thought it would be," Becky said. "The house, I mean. This is the first time I've seen it close up."

"Yeah, and a lot shabbier," Claire said.

"It gives me the creeps," Claire's father said. "Remember when we did the challenge, John?"

Honey's dad smiled, but then his smile quickly turned into something else. Fear? Maybe.

"I remember," John Moon said. "I remember you screamed when that picture fell off the wall."

Mrs. Young laughed. "I think it's safe to say we all did our share of screaming during the challenge."

Honey's dad grabbed her sleeping bag. "And I'm sure these scouts will do the same."

"Maybe not," Honey said. "Kids today are so much more sophisticated. We don't get tricked so easily."

"Who said anything about tricks?" It was Scout Master Matilda on the front porch. She was the only one who wore the scout uniform.

"Hello," Mrs. Young said as the scout master approached.

After shaking hands with the parents, Trout said, "Okay then, don't worry. Your scouts are in good hands."

96

Honey and Becky rolled their eyes, and Claire coughed.

"See ya, Honey," Honey's dad said. "Behave and try to have fun and if . . . well, if something happens, remember, I love you." Then he climbed into the van and pulled away.

"That goes for me too, Slugger," Claire's dad said.

Mrs. Young pulled Becky in for a tight hug. "Have fun. I love you."

The troop watched the parents drive off.

"I'm scared," Becky whispered to Honey.

"Oh, they're just trying to scare us. Look, they all did the challenge, and they survived. We can too."

"That's the spirit," Trout said. "So let's shake a leg you three. Grab your gear and come inside. I have everything set up for us."

A big wind howled through the trees.

"What was that?" Becky asked. "A ghost?"

"No. Just the wind," Claire said.

"Come on ladies," Trout called. "We're gonna have lots of fun."

Honey lugged her gear onto the rickety front porch just in time for a giant wolf spider to plummet from its web above the door lintel. "Eeeek," she screamed.

"Just a spider," Claire said and gave it a swipe with her baseball cap.

"I wasn't really scared," Honey said. "It just surprised me."

"Oh, we are gonna have lots of surprises tonight," said Trout.

All the girls dropped their gear in the huge living room. It seemed this was where they would be spending the night. They would not use the bedrooms tonight, and although she would never admit it, Honey was glad she wouldn't have to sleep by herself. A large stone fireplace was the focal point of the room. Charred wood and ashes remained inside, but Honey knew the fireplace was not to be used. Raggedy, velvet curtains hung from the tall windows, and the cobwebs seemed to be the only thing keeping them together. One dim light shone from a small wall lamp.

"Electricity?" Honey asked. "The place has electricity?"

"Right," Trout replied. "It's hooked up to a generator out back. They mayor had it installed so we could have some light. But mostly we'll rely on our flashlights."

"Wowzers," Claire said, "that's the biggest fireplace I have ever seen. Can we build a fire?"

"Oh, no, no," Trout said. "Too dangerous. The chimney isn't sound."

"But how will we stay warm?" Becky asked.

"Sleeping bags," Honey said. "And it's not

that cold."

A loud clap of thunder sounded overhead. "And as long as it doesn't rain," Honey continued, "we will be fine." She looked around the dark, dusty room. "Just fine." She rubbed her nose. The dust made her itch.

Trout turned the light up in one of the camping lanterns that had been set up around the room. "Thing is," she said, "it seems it always rains on these sleepover challenges. Pretty weird really."

Becky whispered to Honey, "I'm feeling a little better."

"Good. Just twelve more hours to go."

Honey watched Claire swallow like she was swallowing a baseball. "What's the matter, Claire?" Honey asked. "Little scared?"

"No," Claire said. "And I say we explore this dump. Probably some cool stuff around here."

Trout sat in a lawn chair reading a book and not paying too much attention to the scouts. But Honey figured that was all pretty calculated. The more relaxed Trout acted, the more relaxed the scouts would be.

"So," Honey said to Trout, "can we go exploring?"

Trout looked up from her book. She was reading the newest version of the Mummy Mates manual. "Sure, just be careful."

"Aren't you going with us?" Becky asked.

"Nah, I've been through every inch of the place," Trout replied. "You'll be fine. I want to finish this chapter on Internet Safety and the Mummy Mates. It's riveting."

"Okay," Honey said. "Anything we should know?"

"Uhm, let me think. I guess it would be better if you didn't open any trunks or closets—never know what might jump out."

Honey put her hand over her mouth to keep from laughing. She whispered to Claire. "It's obvious she wants us to open closets and trunks."

"Obviously," Claire said.

Trout smiled and raised her eyebrows. "Okey dokey then, have fun. But report back every few minutes, just so I know you're safe."

Honey pulled her cell from her pocket. "Does everybody have full battery?"

"I don't," Becky said. "I forgot to charge it."

"Well, that's too bad," Trout said. "The electrical outlets are not connected to the generator, so you can't plug in a charger."

"It's okay," Claire said. "I brought my portable charger. We have the same phone."

"That's terrific," Becky said. "You're so smart."

Honey looked around the room. Weird

shadows danced along the walls, and streams of light from passing cars lit up some things that might otherwise be unseen, like weird candle holders on the mantel and sconces on the walls. She even caught a glimpse of a wooden gargoyle perched on the stairwell banister.

"Look at that painting," Becky said. She pointed to the portrait above the fireplace. "Is that William Poe?"

"Sure is," Trout said. "Good looking guy, don't you think?"

Honey eyed the painting. Poe was a big man with dark hair, bushy eyebrows, and a beard. His eyes seemed to pierce the air. All Honey or anyone knew about him was that he was wealthy and used to own much of the land that was now Sleepy Hollow.

"Come on, girls," Honey said. "All for one and one for all. Flashlights on. No fear."

104

"Right," Claire said. "It's just a big, old, empty house."

"A big, old, empty house," Becky repeated.

Trout returned to her book and a bag of Cheddar Ghosts.

"Let's go this way first," Honey said. "We'll go upstairs later."

Honey crept down a hallway. Doors lined each side of the passage. A sign hung from one that read "DO NOT ENTER!"

"Geeze," Honey said. "They are going all out for this challenge."

"Come on," Becky said. "Keep going. And turn right at the end."

"Okay," Honey said.

They crept slowly with their flashlights shining on the floor, which was covered in a decaying carpet. It might have been reddish at some point. Honey turned the corner at the end of the hall and screamed.

"What?" Becky called.

"A skeleton," Honey said. "A plastic skeleton on a string."

Claire gave the skeleton a punch. "This might be more fun than scary."

Honey stopped walking, which made Becky and Claire bang into her. "Listen. I know

Clarice is hiding out somewhere, and she won't just resort to plastic skeletons and rubber spiders. So be on the lookout."

"Yeah," Claire said. "She's probably got something much scarier planned."

WHERE'S CLAIRE?

After a little more exploring and not encountering any more surprises, except for one large, real spider, Honey decided it was time to return to the living room.

"Come on," Honey said. "This place is a big bust. A big, fat bust."

"Yeah," Claire said. "It's a fake. This house is no more haunted than my house.

They headed down the long hallway taking their time, walking slowly until another rumble of thunder shook the roof. Lightning lit up the walls.

"Let's go," Becky said, and she dashed down the hall.

"What a fraidy cat," Honey said. She was not about to let something as typical as lightning frighten her.

108

Honey reached the living room. She saw Trout still sitting in her lawn chair. Becky was snuggled in her sleeping bag, but she couldn't see Claire.

"Where's Claire?" Honey asked.

"She was right behind you," Becky said.

Honey looked back. No Claire. Honey's knees felt like Jell-O. "Come on, what gives?"

Trout stood. "Where is Claire?"

"She must be playing a joke," Honey said.

Becky called Claire's name. But her voice only seemed to echo around the large room. Becky called and then Trout called.

"I'll go find her," Honey said. But as she took a step away from the makeshift camp something happened that nearly knocked her off her feet. A small fire ignited inside the fireplace with no help from anyone.

Even Trout jumped back. "What in the world?"

"Aww, come on," Becky said. "It's a trick."

Trout shook her head. "Now that has never happened. It's not on the—"

"The what?" Honey asked with a shaky voice.

"Never mind," Trout said. She stepped closer to the small fire. "It's real. The flames are hot, and it's really burning."

"But you said the fireplace was unsafe," Becky said.

"It is," Trout said.

"You figure this out," Honey said. "I have to find Claire."

Honey started down the hall. She crept slowly, shining her flashlight on the floors, on the wall, and even on the ceilings. When she was about halfway down the hallway, she heard a noise. A groaning sound. Then she thought

110

she heard her name.

"Honey. Honey."

Honey jumped and fell against the wall.
The wall opened, and something or someone
pulled her inside a dark room. Her flashlight
fell to the floor and rolled out of reach. Honey
felt her heart pound like a drum. Her palms
grew sweaty. She wanted to scream. But then
she heard a voice. A familiar voice.

"Claire?" Honey said.

"It's me. I fell into this room, too. I couldn't
get out."

Honey scrambled for her flashlight. She
grabbed it. "Why didn't you call me?"

"I tried," Claire said. "No service. Honey, I'm
scared."

"Don't worry, I'll get out us of here. This is
an old servants' hallway. I just have to find
the same wall panel that got us in here,"

Honey said. "Help me look."

"I looked everywhere. No doors. No windows. Just that creepy, dusty smell and weird noises like rats running along the walls."

Honey shivered. "We should scream."

"I tried. You obviously didn't hear me."

"Right," Honey said. "Well look, like I said, we

just need to find the one movable panel."

Honey reached her hands out and felt along the walls. "Maybe there's a secret button that opens the door."

"There is no way out," a deep, scary voice said from the darkness. "I have you now."

Claire screamed.

"Shhhh," Honey said. She walked toward Claire. "Shhhhhh." Then she whispered. "That voice sounds familiar."

113

"What? Who is it?"

Honey whispered in Claire's ear. "It sounds like Clarice. She's behind this."

Claire nodded.

"Who is it?' Honey called. "Who are you?"

Then there was just tapping on the walls.

Honey whispered, "She's just trying to scare us."

"She's doing a good job."

Honey opened her phone. No service but she tried to send a text to Becky anyway.

"I doubt it will send," she said.

"Come on, Clarice," Claire hollered. "We're on to you. Let us out."

The hidden door swung open. But it wasn't Clarice or Bella Kligore. It was Trout.

"Now, how did you get in there?"

Claire didn't wait around to answer. She squeezed past Trout and into the hallway. Honey followed, and they both hurried back to the living room.

"What gives?" Trout asked. "I didn't even know that room was there."

"Yeah," Becky said. "It's spooky."

Honey flopped down on the ratty sofa. She sunk nearly to the floor. "Like I told Claire, these old houses have hidden passageways. No big deal. There was nothing inside."

"Nothing?"

Claire shook her head. "Just that creeparific voice."

"What voice?" Trout asked.

"I'm pretty sure it was Clarice Kligore. She's out to scare us this weekend. More than this silly, old house ever can."

Trout nodded. "Clarice. She's a pistol."

"But that doesn't explain how that fire got started," Becky said.

"That is strange," Honey said. "But come on. She knows all sorts of tricks, and I bet her father might have helped her or maybe one of his hounds worked some weird magic."

Becky moved closer to Honey. "Hounds? Do you think they might be in the house?"

"No. But I know Clarice and Bella are. We need to be on guard. Don't let anything get to you."

Honey looked into the small fire. "There's a logical solution to every problem and every seemingly spooky trick."

116

The last of the fire fizzled out.

"It certainly didn't last long," Trout said.

"I'm hungry," Claire said. "What's for supper?"

Trout clapped her hands. "I'm glad you asked. We have sandwiches, juice boxes, cookies, chips, and carrot sticks with ranch dressing," Trout said. "We have enough food to stay here a week."

"Oh, don't say that," Becky said. "One night is plenty."

"And don't forget we brought caramel apples and plenty of candy."

"Oooooo, I love caramel apples," Trout said.

The scouts laughed.

"What's so funny?" Trout asked.

"Nothing," Honey said.

Honey unwrapped a ham and cheese sandwich, and then she poked a straw into an apple juice box. "It's not so bad here. Old Poe once had a spectacular house. And we haven't even been upstairs yet."

She bit into her sandwich just as she heard a rustling on the porch.

"Just the wind," Claire said.

But Honey wasn't so sure. It sounded more like footsteps.

118

More To Explore

Supper never tasted so good. Honey ate three sandwiches and a handful of carrots. Then she munched her way through two large, chocolate chip cookies.

"That was delicious," Honey said. "Nothing like a spooky, old house to give you an appetite."

Becky crumpled a baggie and stuffed it into a trash bag. "I could sure go for a caramel apple, now."

"Oh yeah," Honey said. She grabbed her backpack. She looked into Turtle's googly eyes.

"You've been quiet."

Claire laughed. "You and that turtle."

Honey unzipped her backpack and pulled out the container of apples.

"Oh boy," Trout said. "Open those beauties up."

120

Honey lifted the lid on the scrumptious, gooey, caramel apples. She gave Trout the one with the black string. Then she smiled. Honey heard Becky take a deep breath, and Claire was having trouble not laughing.

"Go on, Trout," Honey said. "Take a bite. We made them ourselves."

Trout brought the apple to her mouth. She took a huge bite and . . . spat it across the room. "Yuck. What was that? Ewww." She wiped her mouth on her sleeve. Then she sniffed the

apple. "Onion. It's an onion."

Honey, Becky, and Claire laughed until they cried.

"Okay, okay," Trout said. "Very good. An oldie but always a goodie."

"Gotcha," Honey said.

"Don't worry, though," Becky said. "We

made enough real apples."

Trout was drinking water. "I hope so. But what do you say we clean up and then play some games?"

"Games?" Honey said. "I want to explore. We still have two more floors to get to."

"Yeah," Claire said.

"But Honey," Trout said. "Maybe we should all stay in one place tonight."

"Awww, don't be such a scaredy-cat. This place is harmless, and besides, we have to get to Clarice before she gets to us."

"Yeah," Claire said. "Who knows what she has planned."

"You can count on one thing," Becky said. "Whatever it is, with Bella at her side it will be double the trouble."

Trout tucked the remaining sandwiches into

the cooler. "I don't know, girls."

"Come on," Honey said. "We're here to earn our Courage Badges. Not to sit around and play Chains and Cauldrons. "

Trout shook her head. "Okay. But we have to stick together. We could be in for a bumpy night."

"Fasten your seat belts, scouts," Honey said. "Adventure awaits."

123

After the food and drinks and treats had been put away and the campsite tidied the troop set out to explore the rest of Poe house. Honey knew that Clarice was planning something big. She planned to keep her eyes peeled and her flashlight on. She was not going to let Clarice get her.

"Keep on the lookout," Honey said. "And try not to get scared, no matter what happens."

The troop started up the stairs. A car whizzed

by and shined its headlights on the second-floor landing where a large, framed mirror hung from the wall. Honey tried to resist the urge to look into it as she passed.

"Eeeeek," Honey screamed. "In the mirror!"

"Is it a ghost?" Claire asked.

"Look," Honey said. She stood stock still. Paralyzed.

124

Trout laughed. "Oh, Honey," she said. "It's just me. Old mirrors can distort things."

"Phew," Honey said. "Sorry, troops. Didn't mean to scare you. Forge ahead."

No one else looked into the mirror as they passed. Honey closed her eyes, bent over, and crept slowly past the mysterious mirror. Just in case. Then she crept into the second-floor hallway with the rest of her troop.

"Creepy crows," Claire said. "This place is a little scary."

"Okey dokey, troops," Trout said. "Stick together. Some of these floorboards are a little squishy, and you never know what might be lurking around the corner."

Honey shined her flashlight along the walls looking for another hidden doorway. She was not going to let anyone get caught this time.

The troop continued forward.

125

"I don't think anything is here," Claire said. "Just cobwebs and dust and broken down furniture." She swiped a cobweb away from her face. "I hate spiders."

Honey saw another mirror on the wall at the end of the hall. She shined her light. "Look!" she said. "What's that?"

"A ghost!" Becky cried. "It's a ghost in the mirror. It's standing right next to you."

Honey took a deep breath. She moved closer and sure enough it certainly looked like a foggy, cloudy ghost was inside the mirror. But the closer she got the more she saw it was just a raggedy, old piece of cotton or something. Nothing to be afraid of.

"Just an illusion," Honey said.

Honey turned quickly back, but she didn't see a thing, and when she looked in the mirror again, the ghost was gone. But clearly, someone, and Honey was pretty sure she knew who, was trying to frighten them.

"Well, that was certainly strange," Trout said.

"Strange but easily explained," Honey said. "I bet it was Clarice. She projected the image onto the mirror."

"But how?" Claire said. "She'd have to be behind us to make it work, and she's not."

Honey stepped closer to the mirror and inspected it. Nothing unusual. Just a plain, old mirror with a heavy gold frame.

"Come on," Becky said as she stepped into a large room. "This must have been one of the bedrooms."

"Obviously," Honey said. "The bed is still in there."

A large, four-poster bed stood in the middle of the room. The remnants of draperies hung from the posts. An old trunk sat near the window, which was cracked and broken.

"Look at that," Honey said. "I wonder what's inside?"

"Maybe a treasure," Claire said.

Trout shined her light on the trunk. "I don't know. Maybe you shouldn't open it."

Honey stepped closer. "Oh, c'mon, I bet it's empty." Honey looked at the troop. They all had wide eyes and open mouths. "Here goes." She threw open the lid and screamed. She jumped three feet backward as a large skeleton sprang from the trunk.

The others screamed with her until Trout laughed.

Honey took a closer look. It was nothing more than a plastic skeleton rigged to pop up when the lid was lifted. "Very funny," she said.

"Oh, I don't know," Trout said. "I think it was quite effective."

Claire laughed the hardest. "Now that was

funny," she said after she caught her breath. "I've never seen you jump that far."

"Ha, ha," Honey said. "At least I was brave enough to look inside."

"Now moving on," Trout said, "is the nursery on your left. There's all kinds of scary stories about that room."

"Oooooo, I'm getting scared and nervous," Becky said. "I don't think I can make it through the night."

129

"Come on," Honey said. "You can do it. Just stay with us. Nothing will happen."

After they had explored everything they could on the second floor, the troop headed up the stairs toward the third floor.

"Not much up here," Trout said. "Just a lot of cobwebs, dust, and, oh, be careful, probably mice droppings all over the place. And maybe even some prizes left by raccoons."

"Ewwww," Becky said. "That's gross."

"Power through," Claire said. "It's the only way to get that Courage Badge."

"Okay," Becky said.

Honey was the first to step onto the third floor. The third floor was one huge room, like an attic but tall enough to stand completely straight. Honey headed to the first dormer. She looked out the window and gasped. "What was that?"

Claire dashed to the window. "What was what?"

"I . . . I thought I saw something. It looked like . . . like the Headless Horseman riding across the clouds."

Claire laughed. "Now your imagination has gone completely wild. That is totally ridiculous."

"There it is again," said Honey.

Trout joined Honey near the window. "I don't see anything. Just the moon peeking out from behind those clouds.

"Well, I know what I saw," Honey said. "It was definitely the Headless Horseman."

"Come on," Trout said. "Let's finish up and get back to our cozy camp."

Honey was sure to look through each dormer window. She didn't see the Headless Horseman again, but she was still pretty convinced she had seen something. But how? How could Clarice pull such a sophisticated prank?

"She's got to be hiding around here," Honey said.

"Who?" Trout asked.

"Clarice Kligore and her cousin. I know they're behind these pranks—well, except the skeleton. And I doubt she's done. She's probably waiting for us to fall asleep."

"Asleep?" Becky said. "I don't know about you, but I am not falling asleep."

THUNDER AND LIGHTNING

When the troop arrived back at the living room, Becky was the first to crawl inside her sleeping bag. "I'm staying right here until the sun comes up. This place is creepy."

"Aww, it's just Clarice," Honey said. "She's doing all these tricks to scare us. We can't let her win."

"Sure," Claire said as she hunkered into her sleeping bag. "Nothing to be afraid of. And besides, Trout even admitted to some of the tricks."

Trout turned up the light on the camp lanterns. "A little more light might help." She sat in her lawn chair. "This is when we're supposed to tell scary stories."

"Oh, nooooo," Becky said. "Do we hafta? This place is scary enough."

Honey poked a straw into a juice box. "Yeah. Maybe it would be better to skip the ghost stories. I want to find Clarice and Bella."

"Why?" Claire asked. She munched on boloney. "I say we just let them have their fun and ignore it. Make like we don't even notice."

"I agree," Trout said. "That would probably bother them more. Let them think they didn't get to you. They'll get bored and go home."

Honey wasn't so sure. She wanted to catch Clarice in something. Not so much because she wanted to win but because she thought it might be an opportunity to be nice to her. Maybe by laughing along with Clarice, Honey could get her to see that she didn't have to mean all the time.

"Well, okay," Honey said after a few minutes. "But I'm keeping my eyes open. I think she's got something big planned for later. When she thinks we're asleep."

A crash of thunder boomed overhead.

"Who's sleeping?" Becky said. "I'm staying awake all night."

135

Trout laughed. "That's what they all say."

Another bolt of lightning lit up the room. This time they all saw the silhouette of the Headless Horseman flash on the wall. Honey pulled Turtle close.

"Oh, good gravy," Trout said. "I saw it this time."

"Me too." Claire shivered. "The Headless Horseman. Why is he here?"

Honey shined her light on Claire. "It's just

a fancy trick."

"It's a pretty good trick," Becky said. "It's like the horse is galloping across the sky in search of his missing head. Just like in the story."

"How is Clarice doing it?" Claire asked. She hunkered into her sleeping bag.

"She must have a projector or something set up all over the house," Honey said.

Trout clapped her hands once. "Hey, I brought my guitar. What do you say we have a little sing-along. Nothing like cheerful songs to scare away the things that go bump in the night."

Claire groaned. "No, thank you."

Trout opened her guitar case. "Here's an oldie but a goodie. 'The Wheels on the Bus.'"

"That's a little babyish," Honey said. "We are fifth graders."

"Okay," Trout said. "Then how about 'Bingo'?

You know, B-I-N-G-O."

"Oh, that's fun," Becky said.

Trout strummed her guitar. "But instead of bingo, we'll sing MUMMY. She started singing. After a few bars, Becky joined in and then Claire and finally Honey. And Trout was right, the song did seem to lighten things up. But just when they reached the claps for Y, there came a terrible noise, like someone or something falling down the stairwell.

137

"What in the world," Trout cried. She grabbed her flashlight. "That wasn't supposed to happen. Come on!"

Honey scrambled out of her sleeping bag and dashed toward the stairs. Trout shined her light on the second-floor landing. Nothing there.

"Weird," Honey said. "What was it?"

They heard the same sound one floor up.

"It sounds like someone is running across

the floor," Becky said. "I'm scared. I want to go home."

"Maybe it's the horseman," Claire said, "galloping around."

"Impossible," Honey said. "Come on, let's go up. Check it out. Maybe we can catch Clarice."

"Should we?" Trout said.

Honey shined her light on Trout's face. For a moment she thought even Trout looked frightened. "Yes," Honey said. "You lead."

"Me?" Trout said.

"You are the scout master," Honey said.

Trout crammed a whole cookie in her mouth. "For energy," she mumbled.

Trout started out with the others close behind. Single file.

Step-by-creepy-step they climbed. Becky held Honey's hand. With every step, Becky let out a whimper.

"Shhhh," Trout said.

"Honey," came an eerie voice from somewhere above her. "Honey Mooooooooon- nnnnnnn. Honey Moooooonnnnnn."

"Okay," Honey said. "Now it's getting weird."

The troop stopped as they reached the

139

third floor.

"Honey Mooooonnnnnnn, come forward."

Honey swallowed. She took a step. Then another.

"Don't go," Becky said.

"I have to," Honey whispered.

Honey took a third step. Then a fourth. She felt like she was getting sucked into a tunnel.

"Who is it?" Honey called. "Is that you, Clarice?"

"Honey Moooooooonnnnnnnnn."

Honey's phone buzzed. She pulled it from her pocket. "A text," she said. "From my mother." For a few seconds, her fears lifted. Until she read the text.

At pizza slice.

Just saw Clarice & Bella.

Uncanny

Honey swallowed. Hard. She showed the text to Becky.

"That's it," Becky said. "I'm outta here."

Claire grabbed the phone. "Yep. Me too."

Honey continued to walk toward the voice.

"Come forward, Honey."

Trout grabbed Honey's shirt. "Don't do it. We should just go downstairs."

"No way," Honey said. "I have to find out who it is."

"Maybe it's old man Poe," Becky said.

Honey shrugged and took another step. The others hung back. Honey walked all the way to the end of the room. Nothing. The voice was gone. And there was nothing to see.

"It's a trick," Honey said. "It has to be a trick."

"Okay, good," Trout said. "This was not on the agenda. So let's go back to camp and sing some more."

"And eat," Claire said. "This calls for chocolate chip cookies. Lots of them."

Honey walked back down the hall. She stopped at the middle dormer and looked outside in time to see the shadow of the Headless Horseman in the clouds again.

Her knees buckled, but she managed to pull herself up. "Yeah. Let's just go to the living room and stay there until morning."

Honey snuggled into her sleeping bag with six cookies and a small bag of Fritos. "Okay, okay, so what? My mom saw Clarice and Bella at the Pizza Slice. So what?"

"Yeah," Claire said. "Maybe Clarice set this all up earlier."

"Yeah, right," Becky said.

"Impossible," Trout said. "I've been here all day, and I didn't see anyone."

Honey munched a cookie. "Why were you here all day?"

"Look," Trout said. "The skeleton, the spiders, even the weird ghost in the mirror— all me. I do it every year. I set it up. But that other stuff, the hidden room, the voice, and the Headless Horseman. Not me. Not on the Mummy Mates Official Haunted House Sleepover Agenda."

143

Honey snuggled deeper into her sleeping bag, keeping Turtle close. This was getting weird and scary, but she didn't want to admit it. There's a logical explanation for everything. Honey prided herself on being a good problem solver.

It seemed the house had quieted down, and Honey was getting tired. She yawned and stretched. Becky did the same followed by

Claire and even Trout who said, "Why are yawns contagious?"

"No one really knows," Honey said. "But some scientists believe it has to do with the fact that yawning feels good, and when we see someone else yawn we have an unconscious need to join in."

"That's just weird," Claire said. "Yawns are just yawns. Everybody does it."

144

"And dogs and even fish," Honey said. "And I read one article that—"

But Honey never got to finish her sentence. Another loud bump startled her. "It's on the stairs again," she said. "Same as before."

"Just ignore it," Trout said. "Probably just the wind blowing through the cracks in the roof. Or maybe those loose shutters banging against the walls."

"Maybe," Honey said. "Okay, let's just ignore it for now, but if it happens again, I'm gonna check it out."

"Maybe another song, Trout said. "How about that old camping favorite, 'Kumbaya.'"

Trout strummed her guitar. Claire sang loudest of all, probably, Honey thought because she was really feeling a little frightened. Loud singing chases away the frights, kind of like whistling in the dark.

Honey grabbed onto Turtle and hugged him to her chest. She was a little too old for

145

teddy bears, but Honey figured no one was too old for the kind of comfort she got from Turtle. And to think, there was a day not too long ago when she didn't even want to carry it. Her parents had given it to her as a Christmas gift. Honey thought for sure it was a mistake and that it was meant for Harvest because it looked so childish. But now she couldn't imagine going anywhere without him.

"No fear, Honey," Turtle said.

"No fear," Honey replied.

Honey closed her eyes. She sighed deeply. "Good night, everyone," she said.

"Good night," everyone said.

But, it wasn't long before another loud bump startled Honey again. This time she sat up straight. "Now that was definitely something."

"Yeah, I'll say," Becky said. "It was louder than before. Closer."

"Awww, why'd ya say that?" Claire asked.

"Now I'm scared."

"I'm gonna go check," Honey said.

"No, stay here," Trout said. "I don't want anyone wandering off by themselves."

But when the next bump happened, Honey couldn't help herself. She bolted out of her sleeping bag and headed for the stairwell. She dashed up the steps and just as her foot hit the second-floor hallway she saw the ghost walking down the hall carrying a small lantern. The ghost was eerie and white and mostly hidden in shadow.

147

"Hey," Honey yelled. "Stop."

The ghost moved faster. Honey ran and tackled it. "You won't get away this time."

The ghostly figure groaned.

"Who are you?" Honey asked. "Clarice?" She grabbed the lantern and held it near the ghost's face. It was not Clarice or Bella. Nope. It was Harry.

"Harry!" Honey said. "It was you?"

"Oh, hi, Honey," Harry said. "Surprise."

Honey scrambled to her feet. "Harry Moon. It was you? You did all these creepy tricks?"

Harry laughed. "Well, I had a little help."

That was when Harry's friends, Hao and Bailey, stepped out of a side room. "Surprise," they said. They were dressed like ghosts with sheets pulled over their heads.

148

"Pretty lame looking ghosts," Honey said. "Come on. We have to show the others."

Harry and his friends followed Honey down the stairs and into the living room.

"Look who I found. Our friendly ghosts."

Claire tossed her pillow at Harry. "It was you?"

Becky laughed. "I guess maybe we should have known."

Trout said, "Pretty cool tricks, Harry Moon. I must admit I'm relieved. You really had me going."

Harry and his pals moved closer into the living room.

Becky offered them cookies which they gobbled down.

"Geeze, slow down," Honey said.

"Hey," Bailey said, "playing ghost tricks is hard work."

Honey nudged her brother. "So tell me. How did you manage the Headless Horseman on the clouds?" Honey asked.

Bailey and Hao high-fived. "Yeah, that was pretty cool," Hao said.

"But how?" Claire asked. "How did you do it?"

"Simple," Harry said. "I rigged a projector on the roof."

That was when Honey socked Harry in the shoulder. "Very good, Harry. Very good. Genius even."

Trout strummed a loud chord on her guitar. "Okay, okay, time to break this up. I think it's time for Harry and his little goblins to head on home now. No more shenanigans."

Harry swiped a cookie from the Tupperware container. "All right, all right, we're going."

150

After the boys left Honey and the others climbed into their sleeping bags. Honey looked at her phone. It was 11:30. "I'm tired," she said with a yawn.

"Maybe we can sleep now that all the ghosts and ghouls have been caught," Claire said.

"Okay," Trout said. "Let's all try and sleep."

Honey used Turtle as an extra pillow. "I don't know," she said. "I still cannot believe Clarice hasn't tried anything. I just can't believe it."

A G-G-G-Ghost

It seemed that Honey had just closed her eyes to sleep when a loud BANG woke her. She bolted straight up. "What was that?"

Trout said, "Shhhhhh, listen."

BANG!

This time the sound woke Becky and Claire.

BANG! BANG!

Becky practically leaped into Claire's arms. "That was definitely not nothing."

"Yeah," Claire said. "That was something. Did Harry and his pals come back?"

BANG! BANG! BANG!

"Okay, troops. Remember why we're here. Courage. Everyone just stay calm and quiet. I'm sure it's only the wind knocking the shutters."

But when the next BANG! BANG BANG! happened, Honey said, "No. That was too close."

Becky started to cry. "It's on the stairs."

Honey stood and moved toward the hallway. "No," she whispered. "It sounds like someone or something is running around in the walls."

"A mouse?" Becky said.

"That's one big mouse," Claire said. "More like a phantom kangaroo."

"Can't be mice," Honey said. "Now it's

running around on the second floor." But the instant she said it, she heard the sound close by—in the walls. Then it was upstairs.

Honey looked behind her. Trout and the troop were lined up single file. "I'm going up," Honey said. "There's got be a simple explanation."

Honey headed up the stairs. She tiptoed quietly and stopped when she saw a shadow dance across the wall.

"It looks like a candle," Becky said. "See how it flickers."

"Right," Honey said. "Who would be stupid enough to bring a candle into this run down dump? Harry would never do that."

"A ghost," Claire said. "They always have candles."

Honey crept up the stairway.

BANG! BANG!

Now the sound was below them.

"That ghost sure does get around," Becky said.

Honey stepped into the second-floor hallway. She saw the ghost slinking down the long hall.

"There," Honey said. And Honey dashed toward the figure. "Stop," Honey said.

And in that instant, the ghost stopped and

154

turned. It was holding a large candlestick with a lit candle burning and casting shadows on the wall.

"Come on, Harry," Honey said. "Enough already."

But the ghost turned back and dashed into one of the side rooms. Honey ran after it. She saw it standing near the window. Long, raggedy drapes hung down on either side making the ghost seem even eerier and more spectral.

Honey lunged toward the ghost. The ghost screeched, and the candlestick went flying. It fell to the floor dangerously close to the drapes.

"Watch out," Honey called. "The candle!"

But it was too late. A flame ignited on the drapes. The ancient, worn fabric lit quickly. Flames lapped toward the ceiling.

"FIRE!" Honey yelled.

"OUT," Trout screamed. "Everybody out. FIRE! FIRE!"

Honey grabbed the ghost's hand and pulled. "NOW. Let's go. I don't care who you are."

The troop and the ghost ran out the room and down the steps. They made it safely outside and gathered on the driveway.

Honey could see the flames on the second floor. Some flames were leaping out of the broken windows. "Call 911."

Trout was already on it. "They're on the way!"

"My teddy bear," Claire cried. "My baseball cap."

"Too late," Honey said.

You," she said. "You did this." She yanked off the ghost's mask.

"CLARICE KLIGORE!"

156

TURTLE BLUES

"Clarice, I knew it had to be you. But look, look what you did."

Honey looked toward the house. Flames leaped out of the windows.

"Bella," Clarice cried. "It's me, Bella."

"Bella?" Honey said. "You did this? Where is Clarice?"

"Clarice is still inside." Bella pointed toward the burning building.

"Where?" Honey asked.

The sounds of fire trucks could be heard in the not-so-far distance. "They're coming. But I have to save Clarice."

"She's inside. Not sure where," Bella said. "She might be trapped." Bella started to cry.

158

Trout put her arm around her. "It's okay. The firefighters are coming."

"Was she on the lower floor?" Clarice asked.

Bella sobbed and nodded.

"Okay. I think I know where she is."

Honey took off running toward the house. She ignored Trout's calls to stop. "I go where I am needed," she called. "I go where I am needed."

Honey took a deep breath and dashed onto

the porch. She burst through the door and ran toward the first-floor hallway. Smoke poured down the stairwell.

"Clarice," she called as loud as her lungs would let her. "Clarice."

Honey tapped against the walls. "It's got to be here. It's got be." She kicked and knocked until, finally, she heard kicking coming from behind the wall.

"Clarice," Honey called.

"I'm here. I can't get out. I can't find the panel."

Honey kicked and banged and finally a secret panel opened, revealing a new hallway. She saw Clarice.

"Come on, we have to get out. Fire."

Honey grabbed Clarice's hand. "Follow me."

Honey ran down the hallway with Clarice in

tow. She ran hard as she heard the woosh, whoosh, whoosh of fire above her. She could feel the heat on her face. She ran harder still until they were outside. Honey and Clarice ran, hand-in-hand, toward the troop and Trout who was still with Bella. Claire and Becky stood arm-in-arm crying.

The fire trucks were there already squirting great gushes of water onto the fire.

"I'm sorry," Bella said. "It's my fault."

Clarice broke free from Honey and approached Bella. "What did you do? You ruined everything!"

"Hey," Honey hollered. "Stop it, Clarice. It's not like she set the fire deliberately."

"I don't care," Clarice said. "She still messed up."

Bella looked at the ground. Honey could see her face in the light from the fire trucks. She looked sad and scared all at the same time.

Bella looked at Honey. "What now? Will I go

to jail?"

"Probably," Clarice said. "If my father has anything to say about it."

Honey stamped her foot and glared at Clarice. "She will not. And why are you so mean?"

"Yeah," Trout said. "It was just an accident."

"And besides," Honey said, "she dropped the candle because I chased her."

"So it's your fault," Clarice said. "Wait until I tell my father."

"Hey," Claire said. "Honey just saved your life, and all you can do is yell at Bella and threaten Honey?"

"Yeah," Becky said. "You are the worst kind of bully."

Honey didn't say a word. She just looked at Bella who had started to cry harder. "I don't want to go to jail," Bella whimpered.

Trout stepped in. "You are not going to jail. It was an accident. Nothing more than a stupid prank gone wrong. No one—" she looked hard at Clarice, "is going to jail."

"It was the best prank of all," Clarice said. "But I should have known my cousin would mess it up."

162

Honey had never felt so upset. She had never felt so sorry for anyone as she did at that moment for Bella.

"All right, all right, that's quite enough," Trout said. "I cannot believe you are not the least bit thankful that Honey risked her life to go back into a burning house and save you."

"Yeah," Claire said.

"Yeah," Becky said.

Honey could feel Clarice's glare—it was almost as hot as the fire.

"It's okay," Honey said. "I don't need her thanks. I'm just glad I got to her in that secret hallway. I'm glad I knew about it."

"Secret passageway?" Bella asked. "In the mansion?"

"Sure," Honey said. "All these old houses have them. They were for the servants to use so they could go through the house and not be seen by the family or the family's guests. Kind of weird, really."

"And cruel," Claire Sinclair said. "Wow, who knew?"

"Yeah," Honey said. "It was a little unfair. I mean the servants worked hard, but no one wanted them to be seen."

Honey looked down the long driveway. There was so much more she could say but didn't when she recognized a long, black car pulling onto the property.

"All your parents have been called," Trout

said. "They're on the way to get you."

"Awww, this isn't fair," Claire said. "Now we won't get our Courage Badges."

"Oh, yes you will," Trout said. "And maybe a little extra Hero's Badge for Honey."

Honey smiled. She looked at Clarice who was just standing there looking angry and mean. Honey didn't feel like a hero. She just felt like a kid who did what she had to do.

164

The Phantom Lustro pulled up. Cherry Tomato, the mayor's chief assistant, stepped out. "Oh my goodness gracious," she said looking at the house. "It's ruined."

"Yeah," Clarice said, "thanks to clumsy Bella."

"Bella?" Cherry said. "Oh dear. The mayor is not going to be happy about this."

Clarice stepped toward the car. Bella followed, but Honey grabbed her hand. "It's okay, and you know, the pranks from earlier, with the race and the gum and stuff, that was funny. You guys really had us going."

Bella smiled. Clarice grabbed her other hand. "Come on. Get in the car." The two identical girls climbed into the black Phantom. Cherry Tomato drove off.

"I think the fire marshal will want to speak with Bella," Trout said. "Even though it was an accident."

"Yeah," Honey said. "Funny how Clarice can be so mean and her identical cousin can be so . . . different. I don't think she really liked pulling that prank."

Fire Marshal McCloud approached them. "The fire is under control. Good thing we got here when we did. It could have been so much worse."

"Thank you," Trout said.

"Sure thing," McCloud said, "but I will need to speak to all of the girls and you."

"It was an accident, started when Bella Kligore dropped the candle," Trout said.

"Where is she?" the fire marshal asked.

"She already left," Honey said. "But I was there. She dropped the candlestick, and it landed near the drapes on the second floor."

The fire marshal nodded. "I see. But we'll still need to fill out reports. You understand?"

"Can we do it tomorrow?" Trout asked.

"Oh, sure. Just come down to the firehouse in the morning. It shouldn't take too long. And bring Bella."

Honey and Becky and Claire stood and looked at the house. The top floors were completely destroyed. Puffs of gray smoke continued to burst from the rafters and what was left of the roof. Shingles fell to the ground as a crow flew over, squawking.

"All my stuff," Claire said. "My sleeping bag

and bear. Not to mention the cookies."

"Yeah," Becky said. "My stuff is gone too."

"Me three," Trout said. "My guitar."

Honey let out a deep, sorrowful sigh. "My turtle. I can't believe it."

"Aww, you never really liked that backpack," Claire said. "Now your parents will have to buy you a new one."

167

"Oh, that was before," Honey said. "That turtle has been growing on me. Now I feel sad that he's gone." She shivered when she thought of it getting burned up or destroyed by smoke and water.

"Maybe not," Trout said. "Here comes a firefighter. And she's carrying something."

"We found this on the first floor. Weird, it's in perfect shape. Just a little wet but not even a scorch or soot or smoke damage. Everything else, sleeping bags, backpacks, were destroyed."

Honey grabbed the backpack from firefighter Nan. "Thank you. This is mine."

Honey looked into Turtle's googly eyes. "You're safe. But how? You don't have a single mark." She didn't care that the others looked at her like she had a screw loose.

Firefighter Nan shook her head and shrugged. "Wish I could say how that happened. I couldn't believe it when I saw it sitting there like nothing had happened."

Honey saw Claire sniff back tears.

"It's okay," Honey said. "I think you did a lot of growing up tonight. Maybe you don't need your bear anymore."

Claire nodded.

169

"Honey, Honey."

"Over here, Mom," Honey called.

Mary Moon ran to Honey and gathered her into a strong hug, as Becky's mother and Claire's dad did the same to them.

"You're all safe and sound," Mrs. Moon said. "I was so worried when Trout called."

"We're fine, Mom," Honey said. "Trout got us all to safety. I think I want to go home now."

"Good idea," Claire's dad said. "Let's go, Slugger."

Honey watched Claire and her dad climb into their car. She waited until Becky did the same and they drove off.

"Okay, Mom, let's go home," she said.

But before they could leave, Trout stopped them. "Aren't you going to tell your mother about what you did?"

Honey shook her head. "Maybe later. It's okay."

Trout smiled. "She's a true hero, Mrs. Moon. A true hero."

QUITE A NIGHT

Honey climbed into the passenger side of the minivan. She buckled up but kept Turtle on her lap. She was amazed that his emerald-green shell was still intact and his googly eyes still wobbled. She smiled wide because the longer she had Turtle, the more spectacular he became.

Honey's mom started the van and pulled the gearshift into reverse. She backed slowly around. The car's headlights shined on the building. The firefighters were still working, clearing rubble and hosing down hot spots. Honey burst into tears.

"Oh, dear," Mary Moon said. "Honey. This was a trying night wasn't it?"

All Honey could do was nod her head. Her mom didn't know the half of it. She didn't know that Honey had wanted to help Clarice and ended up saving her life—maybe—at least that's how it appeared. Honey supposed Clarice could have found her own way out or that one of the firefighters would have found her. Still, Honey did go running back inside.

"But it was you," Turtle said. "You rescued her."

Honey took a deep breath and hugged Turtle to her chest.

Honey's mom headed down the driveway. A small crowd had gathered along the road to watch what was happening. Honey didn't know whether to wave or ignore them. She decided it

172

would be best to wave. People might worry or ask questions if she didn't.

"So tell me," Mary Moon said. "What did Scout Master Matilda mean about you being a hero?"

"It was nothing, Mom. But here's what happened."

Honey told her mother the whole story starting from Harry's pranks to the first loud bangs on the ceiling. "And that was when I ran into the house and found the entrance to the secret passageway and rescued Clarice. She wasn't very happy about it. In fact, she was kind of mean and angry. She was really angry at Bella."

Mary Moon pulled the van against the curb and put the gearshift in park. "Wait. You ran back inside a burning building? To rescue Clarice?"

"I figured I was the only one who knew about the secret hallways, and well, I had to Mom. I had to rescue her. There was so much smoke, and the flames were shooting out of the roof. I knew she was on the first floor because that's where the last bangs came from." Honey took a deep breath. She couldn't believe it herself.

Mary reached over and hugged Honey. "I have never been more proud or angrier with you at the same time. You could have been

174

hurt, Honey Moon. Or worse."

Honey shook her head. "No. I don't think so, now that I've had time to think about it. I knew I was covered, you know. Like when Harry says Rabbit has his back. Turtle had me covered."

"You mean you carried it inside and used it like a shield?"

"No. I just knew he was with me. I knew he had me covered. Then Nan, the firefighter, brought him to me later, after they had the fire out. He was completely fine. No burns or scorches or smoke damage. Nothing. He was perfect. Nan couldn't believe it."

"Yeah," Mary Moon said, "he looks just fine. Like new. Maybe better than new."

"Everyone else's stuff was destroyed. From smoke and water and even from fire that fell from the rafters."

Honey's mom pulled away from the curb. "You had quite a night. Let's get home. Dad is worried, and besides, I know he'll want to hear this story."

Honey looked out the window as they passed the park and the Headless Horseman. She smiled when she saw the statue. "Harry had some pretty cool pranks tonight."

"I bet he did. But nothing to compare with what you did."

"Yeah." Honey looked out the window again. "Say Mom? Will you tell Dad the story? I just want to go to bed. I'm pretty tired."

"Sure. You must be exhausted."

True, Honey did feel exhausted. But she also felt sad. Not because the sleepover was canceled but more because of how Clarice acted. She could have at least said, "Thank you."

Honey changed into her pj's, washed her face and hands, and brushed her teeth. She climbed into bed and yawned wide. It had been a long day and an even longer night. She glanced at Turtle hanging from her desk chair.

"Thanks, Turtle," she said.

"Sure thing, Honey. Sometimes I carry your stuff and other times I carry you."

Honey smiled. "Good to know."

177

But as she lay there, her thoughts continued to turn to Clarice and Bella. The more she thought about it, the more she thought that Bella didn't seem particularly happy doing Clarice's bidding.

"Probably bullied her own cousin into doing things," Honey said out loud. "That stinks."

Honey wanted to do something about it. Actually, she wanted two things. She wanted Clarice to at least say, "thank you," and she wanted to get to know Bella a little better. Not that she had much time. There were only two days left of their long weekend.

"What can I do, Turtle?"

"Just be on the lookout for opportunity. It will come."

Opportunity. Honey liked the sound of that.

"I'll think of something tomorrow." And she closed her eyes to sleep.

178

HONEY THE HERO

After church, Honey and her family usually went to Saywell's Drug Store for lunch. But this Sunday, Honey didn't want to go. She wasn't feeling very hungry.

"I'm just too upset, Mom," she said. "I need to see Clarice and ask her why she was so mean to me and Bella."

"Oh, I don't think that's such a good idea," John Moon said. "You could be inviting more trouble or get hurt again. And after the night you had, it might be better if you stayed with us."

John put his arm around Honey and squeezed. "I am proud of you, though. You are a hero. But even heroes need a day off."

"Can I please just go to the park and talk it over with Becky? She said she'd meet me."

But before her dad or mom could answer, Reverend McAdams grabbed Honey's hand. "I heard you were quite the hero last night. That was a brave thing to do."

180

"Thank you, Reverend," Honey said. "But it was nothing, really. I just did what any Mummy Mate would do."

"But how did you know where to find her? Someone told me she was locked behind a wall?"

Honey sighed. "Not really. Those old houses all have secret passageways. I figured she must have been locked inside."

"Well, I think you were quite brave, Honey. Quite brave. And in fact, Mrs. Middlemarch wants to do a story on you for *Awake in Sleepy Hollow.*"

"Oh, my," Mary Moon said. "You'll be famous. At least in Sleepy Hollow."

"Aww, I'd rather not," Honey said. "At least not yet. I need to do something first."

"Oh, that's fine," Reverend McAdams said. "I'm sure she meant to talk to you tomorrow."

181

"Okay, I guess," Honey said. "But right now I need to go and meet Becky."

"All right," Mary said. "But be home later. And Honey, no more burning buildings."

Honey smiled. "Right. No more burning buildings."

Honey dashed off in the direction of the park. She knew Becky would be waiting. Becky didn't make it to church—too tired from the failed sleepover. Honey was also kind of hoping Clarice and Bella would be there. She needed to get to the bottom of things. She needed Clarice to say thank you and to make sure her suspicions about Bella were right.

Becky was on the swings. Honey sat in the swing next to her.

"I still can't believe how brave you were. My dad said you were a little crazy for doing it."

"Aww, I knew I'd be okay. And I knew just where to find her."

"Well, you were still brave." Becky pumped her legs and started to swing higher and higher. Honey joined her, and soon the two were swinging in unison.

"Have you seen Clarice?" Honey asked.

"Today? No."

"Okay, I was hoping she might be hanging around. I want to talk to her."

"Why?" Becky pumped harder.

"I need to know why she couldn't at least say thank you."

"Awww, she'll never tell you. She's just mean, remember?"

"Maybe, but I need to ask. And besides, I want to see Bella, too."

"Yeah, she was pretty upset last night."

183

Honey counted. "One, two, three." She jumped from the highest point of her swing and landed on two feet.

Becky did the same, only she wobbled and fell.

"Come on," Honey said. "Let's go to Folly Farm.

Honey set off walking, but Becky grabbed her arm. "Now I know you're cracked. You're just asking for trouble if you go there. What are you gonna do, just knock on the door? Nobody does that. Folly Farm is scarier than the old Poe house."

"Maybe," Honey said. "But remember, I ran into a burning building. I'm not afraid of Folly Farm."

"Okay," Becky said. "I'll go with you. I don't know anyone who has actually knocked on their door."

Folly Farm was not far. It was where Clarice lived with her father, the mayor of Sleepy Hollow, and her two brothers—they were both bullies, too. Titus was the middle kid, and he pretty much picked on Harry whenever he could. Marcus was older and a senior in high school. What Honey knew about him she learned from talk around town. But Honey was interested in Clarice.

"It's like I've had enough of her stuff," Honey said as they reached the Kligore's driveway. "I'm just gonna tell her how I feel. And tell her to cut it out."

"Wow," Becky said. "This I gotta see."

Honey and Becky started down the long, winding driveway. It was lined with scarecrows and jack-o'-lanterns. Stuffed ravens perched on the fence posts. There were even scary noises rigged up to supposedly scare people —all part of Maximus Kligore's plan to perpetuate Halloween in Sleepy Hollow.

Honey wasn't afraid of the sounds, but she did not like all the Halloween stuff scattered around. There was even a coffin along the way that was being used as a flower bed.

"Good old Sleepy Hollow," Honey said as a raven made a caw caw sound.

They were about halfway down the driveway when Honey heard another noise. It wasn't a crow or jack-o'-lantern. It sounded more like crying. At first Honey thought it was just another Kligorian gimmick. But with each step the sound grew louder and sounded more real than some dumb old recording.

186

Honey looked behind a particularly wide and spreading oak tree. She saw Clarice, or maybe it was Bella. Whoever it was, was sitting with her knees pulled up to her face. She was crying.

"Clarice?" Honey said.

"No, it's me, Bella." Bella looked up. Tears streamed down her cheeks.

Honey swallowed.

"What's wrong?"

"Yeah," Becky said. "What's the matter? Can

we help?"

Bella shook her head.

Honey sat crisscross applesauce next to Bella. Becky did the same.

"It's okay," Honey said. "You can tell me."

Bella wiped her face on her sleeve. "It's just . . . just that I don't like being Clarice's double, her look-alike."

"Oh, really," Honey said. "I guess it could be weird."

"It wouldn't matter if she was nice. But everyone just thinks I'm a bully too. And because of her, I burned down a house. A house. A big, old, special house. Uncle Max was really angry last night."

"Oh," Becky said. "But why do you go along with her? Why do you do mean stuff too?"

Bella sniffled. "Because she tells me to and

. . . and I don't have any other friends in Sleepy Hollow, and whenever I come here, I guess I just need to go along with her."

Honey shook her head. She picked up an acorn and tossed it toward another tree trunk. "No, you don't. Just tell her and . . . and we'll be your friends. Whenever you come here."

"Really?" Bella said.

"Sure," Becky said.

Bella clambered to her feet. "I'd like that, but what about Clarice?"

Honey stood also. "Uhm. What about Clarice?"

"Are you still gonna talk to her?" Becky asked.

"Maybe. But maybe this calls for something more than just talking."

Honey kicked another acorn. This time it ricocheted off the tree trunk and hit Becky's foot. "Sorry," Honey said. "I think we should just go home."

"You're not gonna talk to Clarice?" Becky asked.

"Not yet."

"But wait," Bella said. "Please don't tell her what I said."

"I won't," Honey said. "And by the way, where do you live?"

189

"Oh, I live down in Pennsylvania. Clarice's mother is my aunt. But of course, no one knows about her. No one really knows where she is. Clarice and I are really kind of rare—not too many identical cousins in the world."

"Yeah, that's weird," Honey said. "Makes me feel sad for Clarice. I mean about her mother and all."

"That's why I try and just, you know, humor her. Deep down, Clarice is really not so terrible."

"You might have to look like her, but you don't have to act like her," Honey said.

"That's right," Becky said. "It doesn't mean you have to do everything she says. You don't have to be another Clarice."

Bella leaned against the tree. "I know that now. That fire made me see that. I guess I need to stand up to her too."

"Looks like you could use a Courage Badge, too," Honey said.

"I better get back to the house," Bella said. "Clarice was sleeping late. But she's probably up by now."

"Remember," Honey said. "Be brave."

"Thanks," Bella said. "I'll try."

CONFRONTATION

oney and Becky reached Honey's house in time to see Harry run out the door.

"Hey," Honey called. "Where you going, to play tricks on someone else?"

Harry stopped. "No. I'm going to the Magic Shoppe, and listen, I hope we didn't really scare you guys. It was just for fun."

Honey laughed. "No, not really. The Headless

Horseman shadow had me going a little, though."

Harry shook his head. "Yeah, my projector got burned up in the fire. Dad's a little upset about that."

"Of course," Becky said. "It was on the roof."

"I better go," Harry said.

"See ya," Honey said.

"Okay," Harry said. "And no more burning buildings."

"Everyone says that," Honey said. "Like it happens every day."

Honey and Becky went straight to Honey's room.

"So what are you gonna do about Clarice?" Becky asked.

"I don't know for sure. I was hoping I could

just talk to her, but now, I'm not so sure it would matter."

Becky sat on Honey's bed. "Maybe you need to just forget about it. Maybe no one can help Clarice."

Honey looked over at Turtle. "I don't know. She can't be hopeless. Can she?"

Becky and Honey talked for a little while longer until Becky's mom called.

"I guess I'll see you later," Becky said.

"Sure," Honey said.

Becky opened the bedroom door. "And Honey, I think what you did was very, very courageous. And I'm sorry Clarice is being so mean about it."

"Thanks," Honey said.

Honey spent the rest of Sunday thinking about Clarice. Every once in a while, her thoughts turned to the fire, and if she let herself think about it too hard, she felt frightened. In her mind, she could see the flames leaping out of the third-floor dormers, and she could even feel the heat from the fire. Once or twice she had to sniff back tears, but it was hard to know if the tears were from remembering the fire or because of Clarice.

But she really didn't want to dwell on that too much. It was just so hard to turn some thoughts off. She also didn't really want to be interviewed by Mrs. Middlemarch, not yet anyway. But no matter how hard she tried to concentrate, her mind wandered. Honey wanted to wrap things up with Clarice before she saw the newspaper reporter. She sat on her bed trying to read—she did have that book report due in a few days.

Her eye caught Turtle's eyes. "Then I will feel like a hero. Maybe. If I can help Clarice see that acting mean doesn't make her cool—it just makes her scary."

The next morning Honey headed straight for the playground. She hoped that Becky and

Claire might be there. But it was okay if they weren't.

"Duck!" hollered Claire. She had hit a fly ball, and it was heading straight for Honey's head. She jumped out of the way just in time. The ball rolled under a bush.

"Hey," Honey said. "What did you do that for?"

"It was an accident," Claire said. "I didn't see you coming until too late."

195

"It's okay," Honey said. "Just watch your foul balls from now on."

"How about pitching me some?" Claire asked.

Honey grabbed the softball. "Okay."

Claire stood in a makeshift batter's box.

Honey lobbed the ball underhand. Claire swung and *SMACK!* The ball sailed over Honey's head and landed near the clock tower. "Good one," Honey said.

Honey and Claire both ran toward the ball which was still rolling on the grass. It rolled straight to Clarice Kligore's feet. Clarice was quick to put her foot on it.

"Oh, great," Claire said. "She'll probably steal it."

Clarice picked up the ball. "Hey, nerds," she said.

"Can I have my ball back, please?" Claire asked.

Clarice tossed the ball in the air and caught it. "Maybe yes, maybe no."

"Awww, c'mon, Clarice," Honey said. "Haven't you caused enough trouble this weekend? Give us the ball."

"Trouble? I didn't do anything. It was my dumb cousin. She can't do anything right—except look exactly like me." She ran her hand through her dark hair.

Honey chuckled.

Bella poked her head out from the other side of the clock tower.

"There she is now," Clarice said. "My cousin, the klutz of the world."

Clarice tossed the ball to Bella. Bella missed

191

catching it. Clarice laughed. "See. What a klutz."

Claire dashed past Bella and snagged the ball. "This is mine."

"I know," Bella said. "I was gonna give it to you."

"Thanks," Claire said.

Honey felt her heart pound. She felt angry at Clarice. Not so much for what happened the night before but for how she was treating her own cousin.

"Listen, Clarice. I don't care if you're glad I saved your life or not, but you should at least stop treating your cousin so rotten. She's a nice girl."

Clarice laughed again. This time her laugh seemed to circle around Honey's head like a flock of loud crows.

"You don't tell me what to do, Honey Moon," Clarice said. "Nobody tells me what to do."

Honey felt her hand tighten into a fist. She didn't like the feeling. Oh, it wasn't that Honey never felt angry. She just didn't like being angry, and she especially didn't like it when she thought those feelings could bubble over and create even more trouble.

"But I'm gonna tell you what to do," hollered Bella. "For starters, you can tell Honey what you told me the night of the fire." Bella stepped closer to Clarice.

"What are you talking about, you big dope? I didn't say anything."

"Yeah? Did so. When we got into Uncle Max's car, you started to cry."

Claire Sinclair burst into laughter. "Clarice Kligore cries? Who knew?"

"Did not," Clarice said. "My eyes were just watering from the smoke."

Bella stepped closer. "No. You were crying, and you said how glad you were Honey knew how to find you. You said she saved your life."

Honey felt her eyes grow wide. She could hardly believe what she was hearing.

"Tell her," Bella said. "Tell Honey thank you."

Clarice started to back away, but Bella grabbed her arm. "Tell her!"

"It's okay," Honey said. "I don't need her gratitude. I just want her to stop treating you so mean."

"Yeah," Bella said. "Cut it out. I don't like being a bully. And I'm not doing it anymore."

"All right, all right," Clarice said. "I don't need you. I got my dad's hounds to do my bidding— at least they won't start fires."

"It was an accident," Bella said. "I don't like being a bully. Just because we look alike doesn't mean we have to act alike."

"Whatever," Clarice said. "I can't wait for you

to go home."

"Me either. But guess what? I'm gonna hang out with Honey and Claire today."

"Go ahead," Clarice said. "See if I care."

Bella walked toward Honey.

"Come on, Bella," Honey said. "Let's go to the candy shop. I could use some caramels."

"Yeah," Claire said. "I could use some caramel chocolate bats and one-eyed fish."

Honey and Claire and Bella walked off together.

After a few steps, Honey stopped and looked back at Clarice. She saw Clarice wiping her eyes.

"Is she crying?" Honey asked.

Bella looked back. "Probably."

"I kind of hope so," Honey said. "Maybe she's starting to have some feelings."

"Yeah, but if I ask her about it, she'll definitely say her eyes are still irritated from the smoke."

"Maybe," Honey said. "But we'll know the truth. Clarice got a taste of her medicine today, and it might just be starting to work."

Later that day, Mrs. Middlemarch caught up with Honey at the playground.

202

"Excuse me, Honey. But is this a good time for our interview?"

Honey leaped off the swing. "I guess so."

"Fantastic," Mrs. Middlemarch said. "This won't take long."

"Okay," Honey said. "Shoot."

Mrs. Middlemarch opened her notebook. "So tell me, what were you thinking when you ran into that burning house?"

"I was thinking I had to find Clarice. I was thinking I had to go where I was needed."

Mrs. Middlemarch smiled. "You always do, Honey Moon. Sleepy Hollow can count on you."

Honey swallowed. It wasn't always easy living in Sleepy Hollow, but when it came right down to it, Honey knew there was no better place on earth—at least for her.

Heroic Honey Hurries into Burning Building

Sleepy Hollow—On Saturday night, a fire broke out on the second floor of the old Poe house. The fire marshal told *Awake in Sleepy Hollow* the fire was ignited by a candle. At the time, a small troop of Mummy Mates was in the house for the annual Mummy Mates Sleepover Courage Challenge. Mates included Honey Moon, Becky Young and Claire Sinclair along with Scout Master Matilda (Trout).

According to Scout Master Matilda, there were two other people in the building at the time of the fire. "They were uninvited guests," Trout said. "Clarice Kligore and her cousin, Bella."

This reporter learned that the two uninvited guests went to the sleepover in order to scare the troop. Unfortunately, their pranks went terribly wrong.

It was Honey Moon who uncovered their plot. When she caught Bella Kligore in a ghost costume and confronted her, Bella dropped a candle, and it rolled next to the old draperies in Poe's former bedroom. The drapes caught fire instantly.

After everyone had made it to safety, it was revealed that Clarice Kligore was still inside and probably trapped.

"I knew these old houses have secret passages," Honey Moon said. "I figured she was trapped inside."

Without regard for herself, Honey Moon dashed back

into the burning house to save Clarice Kligore.

"Sure, I was scared," Moon said. "But I also knew I had to find Clarice."

And Moon was correct. Clarice Kligore was trapped inside one of the secret passageways. But Honey Moon got her to safety.

"It was nothing, really," Moon said. "I always go where I am needed."

206

CREATOR'S NOTES

I am enchanted with the world of Honey Moon, the younger sister of Harry Moon. She is smart and courageous and willing to do anything to help right win out. What a powerhouse.

I wish I had a friend like Honey when I was in school. There is something cool about the way Honey and her friends connect with each other that's very special. When I was Honey's age, I spent most of my time in our family barn taking care of rabbits and didn't hang out with other kids a lot. I think I was always a little bit on the outside.

Maybe that's why I like Honey so much. She lives life with wonderful energy and enthusiasm. She doesn't hesitate to speak her mind. And she demands that adults pay attention to her because more often than not, the girl knows what she is talking about. And she often finds herself getting into all kinds of crazy adventures.

We all need real friends like Honey. Growing up is quite an adventure and living it with girlfriends that you love builds friendships that can last a lifetime. That's the point, I think, of Honey's enchanted world—life is just better when you work it out with friends.

I am happy that you have decided to join me, along with author Suzanne Brooks Kuhn, in the enchanted world of Honey Moon. I would love for you to let us know about any fun ideas you have for Honey in her future stories. Visit harrymoon.com and let us know.

See you again in our next visit to the enchanted world of Honey Moon!

MARK ANDREW POE

The Enchanted World of Honey Moon creator Mark Andrew Poe never thought about creating a town where kids battled right and wrong. His dream was to love and care for animals, specifically his friends in the rabbit community.

209

Along the way, Mark became successful in all sorts of interesting careers. He entered the print and publishing world as a young man and his company did really, really well. Mark also became a popular and nationally sought-after health care advocate for the care and well-being of rabbits.

Years ago, Mark came up with the idea of a story about a young boy with a special connection to a world of magic, all revealed through a remarkable rabbit friend. Mark worked on his idea for several years before building a collaborative creative team to help him bring his idea to life.

Harry Moon was born. The team was thrilled when Mark introduced Harry's enchanting sister, Honey Moon. Boy, did she pack an unexpected punch!

In 2014, Mark began a multi-book project to launch *The Amazing Adventures of Harry Moon* and *The Enchanted World of Honey Moon* into the youth marketplace. Harry and Honey are kids who understand the difference between right and wrong. Kids who tangle with magic and forces unseen in a town where "every day is Halloween night." Today, Mark and the creative team continue to work on the many stories of Harry and Honey and the characters of Sleepy Hollow. He lives in suburban Chicago with his wife and his 25 rabbits.

SUZANNE BROOKS KUHN

Suzanne Brooks Kuhn is a mom and author with a passion for children's stories. Suzanne brings her precocious childhood experiences and sassy storytelling ability to her creative team in weaving the magical stories found in *The Enchanted World of Honey Moon*. Suzanne lives with her husband in an 1800's farmhouse nestled in the countryside of central Virginia.

211

BE SURE TO READ THE
CONTINUING AND ENCHANTED
ADVENTURES OF HONEY MOON.

THE
ENCHANTED
WORLD OF
HONEY
MOON

STICKY SITUATION

Suzanne Brooks Kuhn   Created by Mark Andrew Poe

THE
ENCHANTED
WORLD OF
HONEY
MOON

NOT YOUR VALENTINE

Suzanne Brooks Kuhn   Created by Mark Andrew Poe

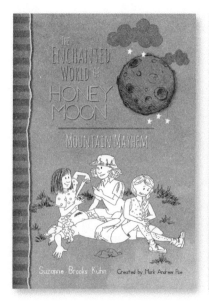

THE
ENCHANTED
WORLD OF
HONEY
MOON

MOUNTAIN MAYHEM

Suzanne Brooks Kuhn   Created by Mark Andrew Poe

THE
ENCHANTED
WORLD OF
HONEY
MOON

SHADES AND SHENANIGANS

Regina Jennings   Created by Mark Andrew Poe